PLOTTED FOR MURDER

ST. MARIN'S COZY MYSTERY SERIES BOOK 4

ACF BOOKENS

1

When Mart dismissed my idea of covering All Booked Up's Harvest Festival float with entirely pumpkin-themed book covers, I knew she was probably right. But it wasn't until I realized that I'd need to scan and then print approximately eighty bazillion covers and then pay to have them blown up to a size that people could actually see from the side of the road that I gave in. As much as I wanted to both introduce people to great titles like *How Many Seeds in a Pumpkin?* and *Pumpkin It Up!*, my favorite cookbook of the season, I wasn't up for that much investment in time or money.

Besides, Mart's idea was much better. Cate, our artist friend, was making a huge pumpkin for the center of the float, and everyone had their costumes all set. The only thing left was to convince Taco that the treats would come to him if he just sat on that doghouse by the typewriter. The problem was, Taco wasn't much interested in being Snoopy. Still, I knew we'd make our Great Pumpkin float work, especially since my boyfriend, Daniel, had agreed to be Charlie Brown, bald cap and all. Mart was going to be Lucy, of course. She had both the attitude and the black hair, and I knew my best friend could be as disdainful as the part required.

I was going to be Peppermint Patty, despite Mart's protests that I should be Lucy since clearly Daniel fawned over me like the Charlie Brown did over the little red-haired girl. But I had been Peppermint Patty's biggest fan since my seventh birthday when I realized she was the smartest and the most laid-back of all the Peanuts. Plus, I sort of already had the hair for it.

This was going to be the first year for our bookstore to have a float in the parade, and I was determined it would win the competition, which was judged by the Chamber of Commerce. The only physical prize was a ridiculous blue bow, but the bragging rights had, I'd witnessed last year, carried the winner through the very quiet days on St. Marin's Main Street in winter. I wanted those bragging rights, and the ribbon would look great in the shop's front window.

But I knew we had stiff competition. Our friend Elle Heron, who ran the local farm stand and a cut flower business, had taken the title for the past two years with her Rose Parade-inspired floats made entirely from autumn blossoms, and despite Cate's willingness to help with our float, I knew the art co-op's creation would be stellar what with all the painters and sculptors involved. Then, when you factored in the Maritime Museum's tall ship made in exactly the same fashion as an actual cutter and the sheriff department's whimsical and totally overblown *Hee Haw* theme, with our African American sheriff dressed as Minnie Pearl, we had to bring our best game.

Good thing my hound dog, Mayhem, loved to wear costumes because she was our pièce de résistance as Woodstock, and I knew the crowd would love our friend Woody as Pig-Pen. He was creating his costume by doing a lot of sanding that day and not showering.

We had five days to finish our float, and I was determined it was going to be amazing. Well, it was going to be amazing if I could actually manage to apply this red paint without streaks. I hated painting, but Snoopy's doghouse was the last big prop for the float. Everyone else had done their part – Woody built the doghouse, Cate was in charge of the "great" pumpkin, Daniel had made a mechanical football to fly over his own head again and again. The least I could do was paint.

Just as I was doing the final trim work around the opening for Taco's very soft dog bed, a necessity if we wanted him to actually make the ride, Daniel showed up with what smelled very much like a breakfast burrito from Luisa Tucker's food truck.

I looked up only to see the burrito waving like a mirage in front of my eyes. It was eight a.m., and besides Mrs. Chevalier's cinnamon rolls, nothing was better for breakfast than Lu's burritos. They were cheesy and spicy and filled with the best eggs and sausage I had ever tasted, and that's saying something because I'm a Southern woman and I know my eggs and sausage. "You sure know the way to my heart, Daniel Galena," I said as I reached up and snatched the burrito from his hand.

"I sure hope so," he said as he bent and kissed the top of my head. "But if all it took was a burrito, I would have started there." He winked as he sat down on a paint bucket next to me. "Looks good." He nodded toward the doghouse as he ate half a burrito in one bite.

"You think so? I feel like it's pretty sloppy." I eyed the streaks I could still see in the bright red paint.

"I think it looks great. Plus, it'll be far away. It doesn't need to be perfect."

I dropped the brush. "That settles it, then. I'm going to silence the ten percent of me that is perfectionistic and let the 'good enough' ninety percent hold sway. I declare this doghouse complete." With that, I tucked into my burrito with force.

After I had inhaled that cheesy goodness, I looked at Daniel. "So what brings you by besides the promise of the sheer joy on my face when you handed me Lu's food?" Daniel and I were together for a bit of pretty much every day, but he wasn't exactly what you'd call a morning person. Most days, he and Taco came by just as I opened at ten o'clock as he was headed to his mechanic's shop up Main Street.

"Taco was lonely." He pointed over to where he had tied up his Basset Hound next to Mayhem on the bike rack at the backside of the alley near an open field.

I grinned. "Oh, Taco was, was he?"

"He was. He misses his girl when he doesn't get to see her for a couple of days."

"Oh yeah? Well, I'm glad you brought him by then."

"How was Mart's race anyway?" Daniel reached into his backpack and produced two more burritos, and my heart skipped a beat.

I kissed him on the cheek as I grabbed my second full meal and said, "It was good. Kind of fun to be back on the West Coast again."

My best friend and roommate, Mart, was a runner. It was a part of our friendship that would never align. I ran only under threat, and Mart ran half-marathons once a month and full marathons a couple times a year. We had long ago agreed to not try to understand the other's running perspectives. But I went to every race I could, and when she said she was going to run the Humboldt Redwoods Marathon in Northern California, I immediately signed on as her roadie.

It had been more than a year since I'd been back to northern California, the place Mart and I had lived before coming cross country to the Eastern Shore of Maryland, and I was eager to visit the eucalyptus forests again. I missed their smell, and I ached for the Pacific Coast with its cliffs looking out over the ocean and lines of pelicans diving into the surf. Plus, Humboldt County was perfect. All evergreen forests and pretty lakes plus just enough town in Eureka to find really good food, even better wine, and some good music, too. We were not, however, going to be partaking in the county's most famous commodity, marijuana, but I did appreciate the mellowed out attitude that seemed to pervade the place.

As soon as Mart had signed up for the race, we'd decided to make it a long weekend out there. We'd been gone since last Wednesday, and while I'd had a blast – including wearing a ridiculous hat with faux fur and dangling bead trim to cheer Mart on as she took first in her age group in the race – I was glad to be back home to St. Marin's. And to Daniel. I'd missed him.

"She rocked it. I think she could have run another 26.4 miles if she'd been allowed," I said. "But by the time she was done, she was starving. You know my favorite meal is breakfast, so we hit this place called The Chalet House of Omelettes."

"Cheddar and mushrooms?"

Oh, he knew me so well. "You know it. But the spectacular part was watching Mart eat two omelets and a short stack of pancakes. For a tiny woman, she can really put it away." I did not miss the irony of the fact that I had just shoved a second, full-size burrito into my mouth while I made this statement, but I didn't care. Lu's burritos were that good.

"Did you make it down to the city?" Daniel looked over at the dogs as he asked.

"Just on the way to and from SFO –the airport, I mean." I leaned over so he could look me in the face. "We didn't see anyone. I did, however, force Mart to take me for take-out at Burma Superstar since it wasn't out of the way on our trip over the Golden Gate. I *needed* a tofu tower and those deep-fried string beans." I tried to make my answer seem light and fun, but I knew there was a lot riding on my answer.

"Oh, okay. I wasn't sure if you were going to spend more time there."

"Nope. I love that city, but I didn't have anyone I wanted to see there." I wiped the paint off my hands and then pulled a bucket up next to him. "You are the only man I want in my life. And I didn't even want that guy when I had him. You don't need to worry."

I had been married when I lived in San Francisco, but that marriage had been broken in some fundamental ways, mainly because the husband in that marriage was broken, so it had ended before I moved back east. But I knew that the fact that I'd been married before was a tender spot with this sweet man I loved.

"The only love I have in San Francisco is that tofu tower. Okay, and maybe the omelettes at Louis's. Oh, and the pork buns from . . ."

He kissed me and then said, "Okay, so my main competition is food. I can work with that."

"As long as you bring me burritos every so often, we shouldn't have a problem," I said slyly as I pushed myself to my feet. How come the ground got lower every time I sat on her? "You're early for the garage. Want to come in?" I pointed toward the back door of the shop.

"Sure," he stood easily from his own paint bucket, and I gave him the evil eye. "How can I help?"

Those four words offered so easily. Oh, they made my heart sputter. "Well, now that you've asked . . ."

While I put the paint away, he got Taco and Mayhem and brought them behind us into the bookstore. They immediately headed to the big orthopedic beds I'd placed in the front window. They were a gift from our favorite customer Galen, who had gotten them through an Instagram deal he was offered by a dog company. The company had hired his Bulldog, Mack, as their spokesdog, and now Mack was flush with merch and ready to share. Dogs in the window were always good for tourist traffic, especially if a Bulldog with a pronounced underbite joined them. During the summer high season, those pups had been all the PR I'd needed for the store.

Daniel had just brought out the last of the pumpkin books I needed for the new window display when Mart burst through the front door. She was sweaty and out of breath, something she hadn't been even at the end of this weekend's marathon.

"Call Tuck. There's been a murder," she huffed out between breaths as she jogged back and forth in the front of the store.

"What?! Mart – slow down," I said even as I grabbed my phone from the counter by the register. "Who's dead?

"Coach Cagle. I just found his body on the high school track."

2

B y the time Mart, Daniel, and I walked the two blocks back to the high school, Sheriff Mason was already on the scene, and he didn't look happy. Specifically, he didn't look happy with Mart.

"What in the world would possess you to leave a man's body here unattended?" The sheriff's voice was low and controlled, but I could sense the anger seething behind his words. He looked like he could chew nails to powder.

Now that she was recovered from the initial shock and fear, Mart was her usual, composed self. "I was afraid," she said with her hands on her hips. "And I thought I heard someone there," she pointed toward the bleachers behind the bathrooms where she'd found the coach's body. "I thought maybe it was the killer. So I ran." She stared at the sheriff until he broke eye contact and walked back to the coach's body.

Coach Cagle was a thin, wiry man – a distance runner all his life, or so I understood from Mart. From Rocky, who ran the coffee shop at the bookstore, I also knew he was a bully. When she'd been in his gym classes, he'd harassed her to no end about her curvy physique. He'd even told her that she'd never find a man if she didn't lose a few pounds. Apparently, Rocky wasn't the only one he bullied, and bullying wasn't the worst of it. There were lots of rumors that he was beyond inappropriate with some of his students.

So I couldn't say the coach would be missed by much of anyone, especially not his female students. Mart only tolerated him because he was an expert at what he did. He'd helped improve her distance times considerably, and she hurt less after long runs. But Mart was also not a teenage girl, and she didn't take crap from anyone, In fact, when I'd told her about Rocky's experience with Cagle, she'd said, "He and I will be having a conversation about this," and sure enough the next afternoon, he'd come by the shop to apologize to Rocky, who, to her credit, had been gracious but cold as ice when she said, "Thank you for your apology. I appreciate that it must have been hard to give it. Take care, Coach."

I had almost applauded. Now, though, with his long legs sticking out of those far-too-short running shorts, I kind of felt bad for the guy. It's hard to find someone despicable when they're dead.

"Looks like it was personal," Tuck said as he bent over the body. "Someone was taking out some anger on this guy."

I started to take a few steps forward to get a closer look, but Daniel put a hand on my arm. "Do you really want that image in your head, Harvey?" he asked quietly.

Immediately, I stopped moving. No, no I did not want to see that. He was right. Instead, I did what my seemingly limitless curiosity led me to do, I asked a question. "You think the person who did this knew him?" I tried to look innocent as Sheriff Mason turned slowly to me, his eyes narrowed.

"I expect so. Stabbings are usually personal, and this," he glanced back at Cagle's body, "this looks really personal."

I again resisted the urge to step forward by feeding my curious mind. "Plus, the person would have had to know he would be here, right?"

Mart spun toward me. "What's that supposed to mean?"

I stared at her for a minute until I realized what my question implied. "No, I didn't mean that, Mart. I mean, since you were meeting him here to train, of course you knew he would be here, but . . ." I petered out. I was just making it worse by trying to explain.

Tucker came to my rescue. "Yes, the person would have had to have known he was here. But from the looks of things, he's been dead a while. I'll know more after the coroner's report, but I don't think he was killed this morning." He winked at Mart. "You're off the hook."

Her eyes went wide with rage. "Well, thank goodness I'm off it since I should have never been on it in the first place."

The sheriff stepped up and raised his hands. "It was a joke, Mart. Sorry."

"You're making a joke about me being a possible murderer? Some joke, Sheriff." Mart's voice could have cut glass.

I stepped between the two of them and put my hands on Mart's shoulders. "It's okay. Let's go get a cinnamon roll," I said. I smiled back at Daniel and Tuck as I led Mart away from the track. I'd seen this sort of reaction in Mart before. It was her post-adrenaline process, and it usually included a fair bit of anger followed by a great measure of tears. Mart was not a person who liked to be seen as weak, and she defined crying as weak. I knew it was better for everyone if we got her to a private place before she broke down.

We just made it, too. I was coming back to the storeroom of the bookstore with two warm cinnamon rolls freshly made by Rocky's mom that morning when I heard the sobs begin. Luckily, Mart was tucked behind the storeroom door at the little table I'd added recently as a sort of break room. "Oh, Harvey," she said as I set the plate down in front of her with a fork. "It was awful."

I sat down beside her and let my forearm rest against hers. "I imagine it was. You knew him, too, so that must have been especially hard."

She took a deep sucking breath. "He was a total jerk, but he was also my friend. How could someone have done this to him?" She continued to cry, but I took the fact that she stabbed the cinnamon roll with the fork and ate a bite as a good sign.

"No one deserves to die that way," I said, "No matter how much of a bully he is. Tuck will figure out who did this. We know that."

She nodded her head ever so slightly as she pried another piece of the roll off. "You'll help him, right?"

Now, it was my turn to be gob-smacked into silence. Mart had always been a staunch opponent of any sort of investigating on my part, so I didn't quite know what to make of her question. "You want me to help look into this murder?"

Mart pushed the pieces of hair that had fallen out of her pony tail from her face and said, "Well, no, not really. Okay, maybe, a little." She picked up the cinnamon roll and shoved the center circle into her mouth whole. "Oh, I don't know. You're going to be involved anyway, aren't you? Maybe I'm just trying to save myself some angst by making myself feel like it was my idea."

I sat back and took a deep breath. "Okay." I wasn't sure what I was feeling just then, a little bit hurt maybe, a lot bit confused for sure. But Mart didn't need to deal with my emotions just then.

"I'll do whatever helps you, Mart. You're always my top priority."

She looked at me out of the corner of her eye, and I saw a little smile turn up one corner of her mouth. "After Daniel."

I blushed. "Okay, after Daniel."

"And Mayhem."

I laughed. "And Mayhem."

"And maybe Taco." Now she was really smiling, and I knew my best friend's equilibrium was returning.

"I'll have to get back to you on where Taco ranks. Remember, he ate my hamburger right off my plate last week. I'm not sure I'm ready to forgive him."

"Fair enough," Mart said as she shoved my cinnamon roll at me. "Now, eat."

I coughed. "I really shouldn't. I had two of Lu's burritos already."

She gave the blue plate a little nudge. "That was at least an hour ago. Be a hobbit. Have a second breakfast. It's your favorite meal of the day."

It was good to be so well-loved. I picked up the roll and chomped down.

MART HEADED HOME a bit later after I exacted a promise that she'd come back at one o'clock and join me for lunch, and I went out to the floor to do the bare minimum of prep for opening at ten. Fortunately, my assistant manager, Marcus, had been up to his usual form while I was gone, and the store was in fine shape. I didn't have much to prepare, so I walked back over to the café so I could chat with Rocky who had seen me come in with Mart and prepped the cinnamon rolls with nary a question.

"Everything okay?" she asked now.

I sighed. "Yeah, she's okay. You'll hear soon, I expect. She found Coach Cagle's body over at the high school this morning. He'd been stabbed."

Rocky's mouth fell open. "Coach was murdered?"

I nodded. "I know he was a real—"

"He was," she said, "but he didn't deserve to be killed. Gracious!" Her face had drained of blood, and she put her hand over her mouth. "Do they have any idea who did it?"

"Not that I've heard," I said. "Tuck was there, so I guess we'll know when we know."

Rocky raised her eyebrows. "You mean, you'll know when you can't resist butting in?"

I cleared my throat and decided to change the subject. "So was it fun for you and Marcus to run the shop together, just the two of you, for a few days?"

My café manager and my assistant manager had been dating for a few months now, and all signs pointed to a long-term commitment sort of situation. They were discreet and totally appropriate at work, but every once in a while, I'd catch them exchanging a glance across the shop floor. There was no doubting this was a big old love thing happening.

Rocky turned her back to me and pretended to clean the milk steamer. "It went great. We work well together."

"I'll say," with as much innuendo as my voice could carry. Then, I laughed, and Rocky turned back to me, a grin across her face as she tugged on one of the curls framing her light-brown face.

"Thanks for keeping the place going. It was good to get away and still know things would be fine here," I said.

"So the trip was good?" Rocky asked, seizing her own chance to change the conversation.

"Very. Mart and I had a blast, and her race was good. Now, though, I have to finish up the prep for the Harvest Festival. I hear it's the big event for St. Marin's in the fall?"

"Yep, the last of the tourists for the season. How's the float coming?"

I frowned. "Just fine, thank you very much. We could use two more Peanuts, though. Sure I can't convince you and Marcus to join me."

She rolled her eyes. "Harvey Beckett, you know there is only one black Peanut. Marcus looks nothing like Franklin, and I refuse to be a token, no matter how good Mr. Schultz's intentions back in the day." She smiled at me. "Nope, we're totally good holding down the fort here."

I laughed. "Fair enough," I said, "although you would make a great Franklin." I turned to open the front door and heard her laughing as she began to steam the milk for the vanilla latte she always made me first thing in the morning.

THE DAY'S sales were steady for a Monday, and, between customers, I kept busy getting the pumpkin display set up in one of the front windows, despite two dogs' commitment to getting under my feet. I even had a bit of time to set up the other window full of October-themed murder mysteries. There was just something about the fall that made me want to dig into a mystery with an amateur sleuth who solves the case.

The centerpiece of that display was Leena Clover's *Apple Caramel*

Mayhem, one of her delightful cozies that included just the perfect number of recipes to make my mouth water. Add to that Samantha Silver's first witch mystery, Lee Child's *Blue Moon*, and Oyinkan Braithwaite's strangely funny novel about a her sister who is a serial killer, and I had a pretty great reading recommendation list for all the mystery lovers in town.

I had just finished putting out the adorable bean bag witches and pumpkins that I'd picked up at a craft fair in September when Sheriff Tucker came in. "Hi Tuck. Cup of coffee?"

The sheriff nodded and headed toward the café as I climbed down out of the front window. I had yet to figure out how to make that exit gracefully, so I almost took out a floor-stand of new bookmarks in my endeavor.

Tuck was already sitting at his usual table near the back of the café close to the counter. He preferred a little privacy on his visits, and I couldn't blame him. As one of three police officers in town, he was often asked to give his ear to grievances about anything and everything. The other evening when he and Lu had come in to pick up a picture book for Lu's niece's sixth birthday, another customer had kept Tuck pinned in the fiction section for twenty minutes as he lamented the excess of stray cats in his neighborhood and the town's need to euthanize "the little buggers." I'd finally had to extricate him from the situation myself by telling him I thought I heard someone trying to break in my back door. The cat-hater tried to follow, but I waylaid him with a diversion to the true crime section. Something just told me this man would appreciate books on serial killers, and I was right. I made a mental note to be sure my cat, Aslan, was kept carefully inside just in case this joker lived near Mart and me.

I sidled over to the sheriff with my second latte of the day and sat down. I'd learned that the best thing to do with most people was to just be present, and they'd talk if they wanted to talk. This was especially true of our usually jovial sheriff on the rare days when he was quiet and introspective. Today was one of his quiet days.

I turned my chair so that I could keep an eye on the register, and then I sat back and enjoyed my drink. A lot of people found it odd that the sheriff came to talk to me, of all people, about his cases from time to time. I wasn't law enforcement, and the sheriff was more than competent to do his job. It wasn't that he needed my help. No, it was more about camaraderie, about needing a sounding board, I thought. As someone who had to talk through things to understand them, I figured the sheriff was probably the same way. He had deputies, sure, but maybe it was safer to just run ideas by a neutral person who was genuinely interested.

It was that genuine interest that gave my friends concern, though. I had a bad habit of getting entwined in investigations, and sometimes my curiosity got me in trouble. I was glad Mart and Daniel weren't in the shop just then . . . but I could see from the look on Rocky's face as she watched us from behind the café counter that she was already wary.

I winked at her with the hope that I could dispel her worry, and then I turned back to the sheriff. He took a long swig of his coffee and then sat back. "Some start to the week, huh?" he said as he ran his hand over his short hair.

"I'll say." I glanced over at the shop. Just a couple of middle-aged women browsing the self-help section. From their careful study of the shelves, I could tell they'd be a while. "Mart was pretty shaken up. I don't know that I've ever seen her that scared."

The sheriff sat forward. "Yeah, that seemed a little out of character for her. She's usually so pulled together."

I looked down into my mug. "Usually. But she thought she heard—"

"Right. I get it. She did the smart thing to get out of there." He looked me in the eye for the first time. "She's not a suspect, Harvey. I hope I don't have to tell you that."

Until that moment, I hadn't realized I was holding my breath, but the wave of relief that washed over me told me I had actually been wondering. "Right. Good. That's good." I took a deep breath and then said, "So any suspects?"

The sheriff squinted at me. "Just between you and me?"

"Of course." I felt a warm body brush against my legs. "Well, you, me, and Mayhem." I bent down to scratch my girl's ear and saw Taco drop his weight against the sheriff's legs. "Okay, between the four of us."

Tuck bounced his foot to give Taco a little nudge. "Too many."

"They're just dogs, Tuck. They can't tell anyone what you say."

He rolled his eyes. "No, Harvey. Too many suspects. Coach Cagle did not have the best reputation, especially with the ladies." His voice was low, but the café was pretty quiet so I wasn't surprised to see Rocky nod vigorously from behind the glass of the pastry case.

"So I've heard," I said, turning my eyes back to the sheriff. "Someone I know had a really rough go of things with him. From what I heard, he should have been fired a long time ago . . . and charged with sexual harassment."

"That's my impression, too," Tuck drained the rest of his coffee. "But impressions aren't evidence, and right now, I'm really short on that essential part of this investigation." He stood up and straightened his gun belt. I always marveled at police officers with all that gear on their waists. It looked so heavy.

"Why's that?" I asked as I stood and moved toward the register where the self-help ladies were waiting with books in their hands as if making their final choices.

"I'm hoping you and Mart might be able to go back to the track with me tonight and see if she remembers anything else, now that the situation is a little less, well, intense." Tuck slipped his sheriff's department baseball cap onto his head. "I thought she might feel calmer if you were there."

I nodded. "So you aren't inviting me along to help with the case?"

He laughed, but then the smile dropped from his lips. "Absolutely not, Harvey Beckett. You're just coming to support your friend. Understood?"

I smiled. "Understood. Happy to do anything for my friends." I waved as he headed for the door then turned back to my customers.

Their choices seemed especially fitting for today: *The Body Keeps The Score* and *Why Does He Do That?*

3

Marcus and Mart showed up right on time at one o'clock, and, after giving Marcus a quick heads-up on the morning's events and urging him to get the details from Rocky, Mart and I headed over to Chez Cuisine for lunch. Apparently, I had not yet had enough breakfast-type food because the cheese soufflé called my name as soon as I saw it on the menu. Mart went with the far more sensible salad with a lemon Dijon dressing that looked amazing.

I had pretty much stopped coming to this delightful French café because the owner, Max, was getting on my very last nerve. He had this fervent crush on me, one he wasn't afraid to flaunt despite my best attempts to put him off and despite his very clear understanding that Daniel and I were together. I missed the food, especially the risotto, but even that cheesy goodness wasn't worth Max's obnoxious flirtation.

Max typically worked nights, though, so I had been hoping that we'd miss him at lunch. Alas, my big mouth and tendency to over-compliment everyone ended that hope when I asked the waitress to thank the chef for the wonderful meal. (It was really wonderful. I could have eaten another entire soufflé if embarrassment hadn't reigned me in.) The eager young woman brought out the chef to meet us since the dining room was mostly empty when we finished, and I was just getting up to shake the young, red-headed man's hand when Max followed him out of the swinging kitchen door.

I had to suppress a groan and force my smile back to my lips as I told the chef the soufflé was the best I'd ever had. Mart chimed in that the salad was perfect and asked about what herbs he'd used when poaching the chicken. This question sparked a lively conversation about the underappreciation of sage which led into a conversation about wine, Mart's specialty. Soon, the two of them had moved off to the wine racks at the side of the restaurant, and I was left there alone with Max.

My eyes darted around the room, hoping the waitress was within sight so I could ask for our check and give Mart the "I'm headed back to work" wave. But alas, the vibrant and eager young woman had disappeared at exactly the wrong moment, and I was forced to stand there and make small talk with my least favorite person in the world. Literally.

"Hi Max." I was trying to be polite.

"Bonjour, mon cher. It's lovely to see you." He bowed and kissed my hand, as usual leaving his lips far too long against my skin. Max was not French in any way. My understanding was that he was Polish, born in Dundalk just outside of Baltimore, and every once in a while I could hear the Baltimore accent creep in. But mostly, he put on this ridiculous affectation of being European, replete with scarves and berets and such on occasion. "If I had known you were coming in, I would have had the chef prepare something special just for you. He makes an excellent apple tart I know you would love."

Now, it was my time to roll my eyes. "I don't actually like fruit desserts very much, and that soufflé was amazing."

"You haven't tasted my recipe for apple tart. I'll make it a point to be sure you can have some on your next visit."

Max had this absolutely obnoxious habit of thinking my personal tastes were something I needed to have improved. Clearly, he had not learned the fundamental lesson of courtship – because that was what he seemed to think he was doing with me, courting. He simply could not cater to the other person's desires rather than try to change them.

Once again, I found myself grateful that Daniel didn't mind at all that I never wanted apple tart or bananas foster or even that cherry ice cream that so many people raved about. He trusted that I knew myself well enough to appreciate cream puffs and white cake with white icing as my natural desires. So much so, every Friday, he brought me two vanilla cupcakes with vanilla icing from our friend Lucas's fledgling cupcake business. Daniel said it was because he knew I needed a little boost after a long workweek, but I also knew he just wanted to support Lucas's new endeavor.

Max would never bring me cupcakes. They would be below him, I'm sure.

I not so subtly shook my key ring in my hands, and then, because I am terrible at small talk and because I just so wanted to keep Max from saying anything else, I began to detail what each key on my ring did. "This one opens the shop doors. This one is for Mart's car. This one is for a car I used to own back in San Francisco. I'm not sure exactly what this one does . . ." After about fifteen explanations, I looked up and hoped to see Max's eyes glazed over with boredom, or even better, to see that he'd just walked away. But no, there he was just staring at me like I was quoting Baudelaire's love poems to him.

Fortunately, at that moment, Mart returned to the table with the chef. "Harvey, this is Symeon. Symeon Cagle." She leaned hard on the last name.

"Oh. *Oh.* Nice to meet you, Symeon." I glanced at Max, who looked quite peeved that our "conversation" had been interrupted. I chose to ignore him by putting my foot in my mouth, not an unusual occurrence. "Are you related to Coach Cagle?" I have all the tact of a lion with a raw steak.

I saw the corners of his eyes pinch, but he smiled at me. "Yes, Coach was my uncle. Terrible thing that happened to him. I guess you guys heard?" He looked from me to Mart and then over to Max.

Max blew me a kiss and walked away without a word. Apparently, the news of a murder did not warrant the same attention as the uses of my keys. I resisted the temptation to try to explain Max's gesture to this man I had just met and said, instead, "I'm so sorry for your loss."

Symeon nodded. "Thank you. I appreciate that, and any death is a horrible thing, but to be honest, I didn't much like him. Nobody did really. He was a jerk to most people." He tilted his head and looked from me to Mart again. "Has news spread that quickly? I mean St. Mariner's love nothing more than gossip, but even this feels pretty fast—"

Mart cut him off. "I'm actually the one who found him. He was my running coach."

This time Symeon's wince was more intense. "Oomph. Sorry."

Mart sighed. "He was a good coach."

"I had heard that," Symeon said. Then, there was this gigantic awkward pause, a pause so big that tractor trailers could have driven through it.

It was into that gaping hole of silence that I realized that I might need to say something. "Well, anyway, I just, well, lunch was really good." One would think that after all the books I'd read I could come up with a better compliment than *good* but there we were.

Symeon grinned. "I'm glad you liked it, and I'm glad you braved the, er, atmosphere to come in." He winked and threw a glance back to where Max hovered by the pass-through window into the kitchen. "You two are brave."

"Hey, we don't work here," Mart said with a laugh as we headed toward the door.

Once we were on the street, I groaned. "Now what do we do? The food is great, and the chef is nice . . . but Max. That man!"

Mart slipped her arm through mine. "He is something." She glanced back through the window one more time. "Might be worth the trouble though."

I smiled.

MART WALKED me back to the shop and then headed out for her job at the winery. Some days I envied her because she got to jet off to wineries all along the east coast to consult, and on the days when her full-time job was winery manager, her hours were always at her discretion. She was that good.

I watched her stroll up the street toward her car and felt a little jealous, but then, I walked in the bookstore, heard that little bell over the door ring, and took a deep breath. Nothing gave me as much peace as the scent of paper and coffee. It smelled like home.

Behind the register, Marcus was just putting a copy of *The Complete Illustrated Book of Herbs* into a customer's reusable bag, and as she walked toward me to leave the store, he rolled his eyes. "I never knew there was so much to know about the uses for thyme."

"I bet you do now, though, huh?" Our customers were always eager to expound on their loves, and nothing gave people more license to talk about their passions than a new book on the subject. Well, nothing except a well-placed question. "Any tips?"

"I tuned out sometime around the part about fresh leaves in a rolled pork roast, but that did sound delicious." Marcus smacked his lips together.

My assistant manager was an ideal co-worker. He was never late. He knew his subject, and he loved talking with customers even more than I did. Except, it appeared, when it came to culinary herbs. Before I'd hired him, Marcus's reputation in town had been a bit marred – some by the fact that he'd stopped college and some by the racism that came with the fact that he was a Black man. But now, after he'd personally recommended a book to almost everyone in town with great success, he was one of the reasons people came to my store.

He was also the reason I could take long lunches and got an occasional day off. His mom also wrote a book matchmaking article in our newsletter, and much like Tannie Maria in the wonderful South African murder mysteries by Sally Andrew, she was a natural. We sold more books off her recommendations than on even my most eye-catching window display. I owed a lot to the Dawson family.

Just then, the bell rang over the door, and a white woman with very tan skin and the longest, thinnest arms and legs I'd ever seen headed toward the sports section. Given my recent weekend at the Humboldt Marathon, I recognized a runner when I saw one, and this woman was a serious runner. I gave her a few minutes to browse on her own just in case she'd come in looking for something specific that she could grab easily, but when she lingered by the two shelves of running books we stocked, thanks to Mart's suggestions, I headed over. "Help you find anything?"

The woman turned toward me. Her face was pinched, like she'd pulled a muscle, but she smiled when she met my eyes. "I'm not sure. I've got terrible shin splints for the first time in my life, and I was hoping you might have a book about stretches or technique or something."

I was way out of my element and wished Mart had come in with me before she headed off to work, but I scanned the shelves anyway. I had some flicker of a memory about a book Mart had suggested, something with a teal cover. Yep, there it was. I grabbed the copy of *Running Rewired* and held it up. "Something like this?" I pulled my mouth into a smile mixed with a cringe. "I'm not much of a runner, but my best friend thought this one had good resources. She's a marathoner."

"Oh, cool. Does she live nearby? Maybe I know her."

"She does. We're roommates. Mart Weston?"

The woman looked past my shoulder for a second as if thinking about something before meeting my gaze again. "Sorry, don't think I know her. Does she train in the area?"

Before I thought I said, "Oh yeah, Coach Cagle over at the high school—" I stopped mid-sentence, remembering the man had just been killed.

"Oh, I know Coach, alright, but I don't train with him anymore. How does – Mart, is that right? – how does she like him?" She was staring hard at an illustration of a hamstring, and I got the impression she didn't want to make eye contact.

I sighed. I might as well tell her because the St. Marin's gossip train would reach her anyway. "I guess you haven't heard yet?"

She frowned. "Heard what? He didn't harass some woman again, did he?"

I shook my head. "No, actually, he was murdered."

She sucked in a breath. "Holy crap. No, I hadn't heard that. Wow." She kept staring at the illustration. "Man." She shook her head a little bit but then looked back at me after letting out a hard breath. "The guy was a jerk but . . ."

"Yeah." I looked from the book to her face. "Anyway, if there's anything else you need, we're right over there. Just let us know."

She glanced over at the counter. "Thanks. Oh, and I'm Tiffany Steinburg. Nice to meet you." She smiled warmly as she put out her hand. "This place is great."

"Nice to meet you, Tiffany. I'm Harvey Beckett. This is my store."

Tiffany looked around. "My first time in, but I like it. And this," she waved the book, "looks perfect. If it's okay, I'd like to take a look."

"Please do. Customers are always welcome to browse."

She waved as I headed back to the counter to take a gander at the day's sales so far.

A FEW MINUTES LATER, Elle Heron from the local farm stand stopped by with two buckets of cut flowers. Each week, she delivered new stems for the tiny vases on the tables in the café, and recently, I'd added an order for a big bouquet to put on the front desk. I knew most people thought of flowers as spring-time things, but the fall colors – the sunflowers and late dahlias, even the weird green seed pods that Elle called "hairy balls" – made me happy.

"Oh, those look incredible, Elle. What are these?" I asked as I lifted flowers that looked like Dr. Seuss's Christmas trees.

"Celosia," Elle said. "They're just so perky and bright."

I nodded. I loved all the reds and yellows. "These will be perfect for the tables."

"Yep, and this batch is for you." Out of one bucket, she lifted a perfectly-arranged group of sunflowers in the most brilliant golds and oranges I'd ever seen. She slipped them into the green glass vase I had washed earlier for this very purpose, and they made the entire counter look more happy.

"Oh, I LOVE them, and you know Daniel's favorite flowers are sunflowers." I blushed a little at my impromptu confession.

"Well, then these should make him even sweeter on you than he already is, if that's even possible." She batted her eyes at me and put a finger in her cheek before she turned toward the book-shelves behind her. "Mind if I take a look at your business section. I have an idea for expanding my market share, but I want to be sure I revise my business plan before I go too far."

I smiled. "Sure. You know where the business section is, right?"

"Yep." She headed right toward it.

That was one of the reasons I loved Elle – she was a fellow busi-nesswoman, and, like me, she was always looking for ways to improve her cash flow while also serving her customers better. The difference between Elle and me was that she loved a written plan, and I loved to wing it. Both of us had done alright so far, so I took that as yet another sign that it takes all kinds in the world.

As I ran a quick report on the morning's sales, Marcus returned from the café with two mugs of steaming hot tea, for which I was mighty grateful. I'd have preferred a latte, but even a decaf one might have too much caffeine for my middle-aged body. I loved sleep too much to risk it.

"I thought yours smelled so good that I couldn't resist," Marcus said as he sipped from his own mug. "Can you smell it?"

I could. Cinnamon and something sweet. "Is that nutmeg?"

He winked. "You'll like it."

I took a little sip, and grinned. "Seriously, pumpkin tea? I didn't even know that was a thing." I perched myself on the stool behind the counter and took another sip. "It's just a little sweet, but I don't taste sugar.

"Nope. No sugar. The tea shop I get it from up in Easton doesn't sweeten their blends," Rocky said as she hopped up on the counter beside Marcus. "But the owner said that she thinks it's the blend of spices that make people think it's sweetened, like a pumpkin pie."

"Well, I'll take the illusion of sweetness without the calories. No problem there," I said.

"Good because I brought in a bunch more of her teas, too, and she's going to be here in the café on Saturday to do a demo of how to brew loose tea well. Hope that's okay." Rocky looked at me over the rim of her own mug.

"More than okay. I love that. I never have been able to figure out how to use an infuser without leaving bits of tea in the mug. Those little sprigs get caught in my teeth. I hate that more than I hate pulp in orange juice."

"You hate pulp in orange juice?" Marcus asked. "What is it? Too much like an actual orange."

"Precisely. I don't like oranges either." I laughed and then watched Elle come back to the counter, a book in her hand and a frown on her face.

She gave a subtle swing of her head back toward the direction from which she's come then asks, "You know that woman over there? The thin one?"

I catch a glimpse of Tiffany's legs and say, "Just met her. Tiffany Steinberg. Apparently, she's a runner."

Elle took out her debit card as I rang up her book, with the employee discount of course. "That makes sense then. She was just talking with someone about Coach Cagle."

"Oh yeah, she knew him, I guess. But pretty much everybody's talking about his murder, right? Something else?" Elle was still frowning, and I knew my friend well enough to recognize when something was troubling her.

"I'm not sure. She was saying that she was glad somebody took care of him. 'He got what he deserved.' That's what she said." Elle shrugged and shimmied her shoulders. "I don't disagree, but something about how she said it."

I pursed my lips and leaned over to see more of Tiffany in the wing chair. She was reading again, so it wouldn't do me any good to eavesdrop by pretending to straighten the books there.

"Maybe he harassed her," Rocky said. "If someone had been harassing me, scaring me like Coach did a lot of women, I'd probably be relieved if he was dead."

Elle shrugged again. "Yeah, maybe." She smiled. "Well, thanks for the book, Harvey. Rocky, Marcus, good to see you, too."

"You'll let us know about this new angle of the business?"

"As soon as I get the details in place, you'll know. Trust me." She winked as she slipped her book under her arm.

Ooh, another mystery, I thought.

4

On Tuesday morning when I got to the store to open, a huge, wooden, flat trailer was parked in the alley behind the shop. The float had arrived.

Daniel nearly scared me out of my skin when he dropped an arm around my shoulder as I stood by the trailer, a bit flabbergasted.

"Sorry," Daniel said as he bent to kiss my cheek after I had jumped nearly high enough to clear the trailer. "Didn't mean to startle you. You were really concentrating there. Brainstorming how to decorate?"

I looked from him to the trailer and back again. It was so big, and I didn't know if our doghouse, the shrubs that the garden center next door were loaning us, and our scant cast were going to fill it enough. We might look far more like Charlie Brown's Christmas Tree than I wanted. I mean, I appreciated the symbolic nature of the cartoon, but on a float – we might just look cheap or even worse – uncreative. "More like trying to decide how many pumpkins I can buy to fill her up. Does that stand out by the highway still have a lot of them? Maybe I can buy their old ones, the ones that are starting to go? I don't think I can afford to buy dozens of fresh pumpkins, but the slightly rotted ones will look okay if we pile them up, right? Or maybe I can make a whole bunch from papier-mâché? I can go a couple nights without sleep—"

"Whoa, Harvey. Take a breath. We're okay. The float will look great. You and Mart have done a great job designing it. And look," he pulled a bright yellow T-shirt out from behind his back, "I have my costume well in hand."

I stared at the shirt and said, "It's not striped." I felt my panic starting to rise again.

"That's what this is for." He held up a fat, black marker.

"You're going to draw the stripes? What if you—"

"And this," he said as he drew a ruler out of his back pocket. "It'll be perfect, Harvey. Besides, it's the local parade. We're not passing in front of Macy's or anything . . . unless of course there's something you haven't told me yet." He feigned a look of panic by making his eyes wide and dropping his jaw. "We aren't going to New York are we?"

I punched him lightly in the stomach. "No. I just," I sighed, "I just want it to look good. It's advertising, but more, I don't want to let the town down."

Daniel snorted with laughter. "Harvey, the last thing you could do is let this town down. Your events bring new people all the time, and the number of fundraisers you've done for folks hasn't gone unnoticed." He drew me against his chest. "Honestly, I think you could probably walk down the street reading *Harry Potter* and people would still cheer."

I squeezed him and then took a step back to look into his face. "Okay, I'll stop fretting. Thanks. But maybe I should get a few pumpkins?"

"Fret not. Let me take care of any pumpkin-related needs, okay?" He pointed to the doghouse. "For now, let's work on getting this up there."

We spent the next few minutes hefting the doghouse – okay, Daniel did the hefting, and I supervised –and putting it into position. It took up a good quarter of the flatbed, and I could see we would be fine. I did jot down "yellow and orange streamers" on the palm of my hand, though. The sides needed something.

"I don't know if you've heard, but there's this invention called paper." Cate's voice echoed off the back of the store as she walked up the alley. I could see her car down a ways, behind the art coop she ran.

I looked at my hand and then at my dear friend. "I've heard of that material. Flat. Often white. Porous."

"That's the one." She gave me a hug. "Seriously, Harvey, just put a notebook in your pocket."

"Why didn't I think of that?" I rolled my eyes. "You know, I've tried over and over again to carry a notepad with me, but I always end up setting it down somewhere. But my skin, it's always here."

Now Cate rolled her eyes and turned to look at the float. "That doghouse looks great. How does Mayhem like it?"

My pup lifted her head from the patch of grass she'd claimed when we'd arrived and looked less than stoked by the idea of a doghouse. Beside her, Taco snored from his completely prone position with his butt against her back.

"You actually think she's going to sleep in a doghouse?" Daniel said. "Only if Harvey puts it on her own bed inside the house."

Cate laughed. "You're one to talk, Mr. Bassett-Hound Sofa Man."

Daniel puffed out his chest. "Taco is a fragile flower." He laughed. "Mind if he spends the day, Harvey?"

I looked over at the two dogs who were now making a perfect T in the grass with their bodies, smiled and said, "I don't know. He might be a handful."

"Only if you try to pick him up," Daniel said over his shoulder as he headed down the alley. "Lunch?"

"Perfect. Lu's got a new mole sauce I want to try." Ever since we'd been dating, Daniel and I had been meeting for lunch at Lu's lunch truck. He'd introduced me to her tacos on one of our first dates, and I wasn't willing to swear that his taste in food wasn't what had made me fall in love with him.

Cate helped me coax the two hounds into the back door of the shop, and once in, they headed right to the front window, where their matching dog beds were waiting. I didn't complain. We'd had more than one new customer come in because of the cute puppies in the window.

"What brings you by on this fine morning, my friend?" I asked as I logged into the register and then moved to the back of the store where Rocky was already brewing coffee in the café.

"I saw the trailer and wanted to get a sense of scale for the pumpkin. I'm going to start it tonight." She tucked her small frame into a chair by the window and flipped her sleek black hair behind her ears.

I took a deep breath, but I still heard the squeak in my voice as I sat down across from her and said, "You haven't started yet?"

Cate laid her hand over mine. "Don't worry. Lucas built the frame over the weekend. I'll do a few layers each night and paint it on Friday. We'll be ready in plenty of time for Saturday. papier-mâché is really easy."

I shivered as I remembered my attempt to make a piñata for my own thirteenth birthday. All that had resulted was a big pile of rock-hard newspaper that my mom had needed to help me pry off our dining room table. "Easy for you, maybe?" I said.

"I am an artiste," Cate said with a laugh. My friend was a very talented photographer, but she had none of the pretention that so many people think artists carry. If anything, she was one of the most down-to-earth people I knew. She squeezed my hand. "I also wanted to see if you're still game to try the new hair salon in town. I'm going this afternoon, and I booked you an appointment, too, just in case you could get off."

I laughed. "You're very optimistic." I frowned. "Or you really think I need a haircut." I had a thick mop of hair that required a drastic amount of pomade, a kerchief, or a baseball cap to tame.

"You know I love your curl." Cate reached up and tugged on a lock that was dangling over my left eye. "My parents gave me many things, but fun hair is not one of them."

I laughed. "I would love to have your hair. It's so—"

"Straight. Boring. There are many great things about my Korean heritage, but I wouldn't rank my hair as one of them." Cate flipped her hair back, and it fell into the exact position it had been in before.

If I did that, I'd have some rogue curl flinging wildly in the air. On rare days, I loved my hair, but today was not one of those days. And I definitely needed a haircut. Right now, the sides were puffing out and making my hair look a third bigger than it was. "I'm in. What time?"

We made plans for our haircuts at three p.m., and Rocky sent Cate out with a big mug of coffee and a cinnamon scone. I followed her to the door to turn on the neon open sign and to greet Galen and Mack on their weekly visit to the bookstore.

Mack took a hard left as soon as he was in and nestled himself – with a bit of brute force – between Mayhem and Taco in the window as Galen headed back to the mystery section with a big wave. Not many men read cozy mysteries, but Galen did – voraciously. That man could finish a novel a day most weeks, and he was, hands-down, my best customer, even without his continual promotion of the shop on his Instagram feed.

I waved back and then headed to the front of the store to snap a picture of the dogs for our own Instagram page. Our likes always climbed when I tagged Mack. Someday, we might have as many followers as the Bulldog, but not any day soon.

A few minutes later, Galen came to the counter with his usual stack of titles. "This one is for you." He handed me a small paperback book with brightly colored yarn on the cover. "I mean for you to read. Obviously, it's yours since you own it." The wrinkles at the corners of Galen's gray eyes got deeper in his white skin. The man is probably close to seventy-five, but he hasn't lost any of the spring in his step. "The sleuth reminds me of you."

A groan sounded somewhere over my shoulder, and I looked back to see Marcus standing behind me. "Harvey does not need any encouragement in the sleuthing department. I thought you knew that, Galen." Marcus was smiling, but there was a serious undertone to his words.

"Oh, it's not the sleuthing I'm thinking of – although now that you mention it." He winked at me. "No, she's a business owner in a small town, or at least she becomes one." Galen winced. "Sorry. That's a small spoiler, but the book is still good."

"*Yarned and Dangerous.* Sounds fun. Thanks, Galen. I'll give it a read."

"Good. And then write the author and tell her we need more

books in this series. There are only two, and I'm aching for more."

I laughed. "Ah, so you're just using me for your own bookish ends."

"You bet I am, Ms. Beckett. I have to get my book fix whatever way I can." He slid the rest of the stack – maybe ten books – toward me. "These, however, are for me to take home."

I glanced at his titles. Mostly mysteries but a couple YA fantasy titles, too. "I didn't take you for a *Ghost Academy* reader, Galen." I'd read the books a couple of weeks earlier and reviewed them on my Goodreads feed, but they weren't to everyone's taste.

"Believe it or not, I read most of the things you recommend, Harvey, even books about ghosts who have to go to school."

I cackled. "I'll take that as a high compliment." I bagged his purchases and then handed him a dog treat. "Rocky has started offering doggy goodies in the café. She wanted Mack to be the first to sample her latest – pumpkin cookies."

Galen waved the cookie in the air, and as if by some sort of psychic sense, Mack lifted his head and then lumbered over. Without hesitation, he ate the whole thing in one bite. "Mack approves," Galen said to Rocky as he headed her way. "Let's do a photo of those, shall we?"

Rocky laughed. "I'd be honored."

By some great gift of fortune or friendship, Lu parked her truck right in front of the shop for the lunch rush, and Marcus and I had our hands full for the late morning and early afternoon as customers decided to browse our shelves before or, it appeared from the greasy fingerprints on the front door, after they sampled Lu's delicious offerings.

Fortunately, though, the crowd thinned by the time Daniel arrived, and the warm sun made it possible for us to eat our tacos on a bench just up the street. It was one of those autumn days where everything felt perfect. The sunlight was that particular shade of gold that only comes in the autumn, but the breeze carries with it the scent of leaves and last night's wood fires. "This day is perfect," I said as I leaned back and rubbed my stomach, now full of Lu's new chicken with mole tacos. "I could live a year of days like this."

Daniel sighed. "I know what you mean, but don't you think maybe it's particularly amazing because we don't have a year full of these kind of days. They might not be so amazing if we didn't have the skin-boiling heat of late August or the near-freezing rainy days of March, right?"

I sighed. "You may be right, but today, I'm going to pretend I'd like every day to be this way." I sat up and stretched my arms above my head just as a group of joggers passed by in the bike lane on Main Street. "I know I'm not a jogger, but I don't think I'd choose to run on this road."

"It is a little tight," Daniel agreed as he reached down to pat Taco's belly. The Basset was stretched full-length beneath the bench, and Mayhem was resting against my shins. "But you know that for some people, exercise is a spectator sport."

I guffawed. "You mean the way I do it? As a spectator."

Daniel grinned. "No. I mean that some people run or bike or lift weights by the windows of the gym so that people will notice. It feeds their ego."

I rolled my eyes. "I guess, but it's hard for me to imagine. I prefer no one see me all sweaty and red-faced myself, but then, I don't look like that when I run." I pointed at a tall, blonde woman with long legs fairly gliding down the road.

"I wouldn't know. I haven't had the pleasure."

"And be glad of that because as I've said, if I'm running, it's because something is after me."

Daniel helped me to my feet. " Word has it you're in for a haircut today."

I threw my head back. "I can't believe it. The gossip mill of St. Marin's even has the chain going for a haircut."

"You, my dear, are often the talk of the town." He flipped my hand into the crook of his arm and then bent to pick up the dogs' leashes. "But this time, I think it's the where of your styling that is big news."

I stopped. "Why? Is this stylist infamous for shaving random stripes in your hair?"

"Oh, nothing like that. He's really good. Just, well, unconventional for St. Marin's."

I took a step back. "You're not going to tell me, are you?"

"Nope. Some things are better as surprises. Stop by the garage when you're done. I can't wait to see how Scott works his magic on you."

I started walking again and huffed as I went. "So you think I need a new haircut, too?"

Daniel put both hands up in front of his chest. "I never said that. You always look amazing." He held my gaze to affirm that he meant what he said. "I'll just say this, Scott is to hair what an expert pin-striper is to a hot rod."

I groaned. "Like I'm going to get a car metaphor. Thanks a lot." But I was laughing. All this mystery was actually getting me a little excited about the appointment. Daniel laughed too as he handed me Mayhem's leash and headed toward the garage with a smile.

AT TWO THIRTY, I waved to Marcus and headed down the street with Mayhem to the art co-op. I'd told Cate I'd meet her there because she said the new salon was closer to her place than mine. As I walked, I saw Elle outside her farm stand. She had sawhorses and some long boards in front of her. I waved, and she lifted a quick hand in front of her before dropping her head and starting up the circular saw. Clearly, she was focused on her project. I wondered if all that wood-working had to do with her new business venture, and I was curious about why she hadn't asked our friend Woody, an expert carpenter, to help her with her project. I sighed and pushed down my curiosity. I'd find out what I needed to know when I needed to know it . . . or when I found a subtle way to get more information.

I walked the next couple of blocks brainstorming what books I might order and give to Elle to spark a conversation about her new project. My friends were right. I was downright nosy, so why not embrace it?

As I walked up to the co-op, I lost all track of my nosy conniving when I saw the storefront next to art studios. Hanging from almost invisible lines were several dozen hand mirrors. Each of them was unique – some painted bright reds or purples and others the original gilt of silver or gold. They hung from the base of the window to the top, and I was mesmerized by their spinning and the way they reflected light into the shop behind them and out onto the street, too.

I felt a hand slip around my waist. "Amazing, isn't it? Scott's got a flair for the visual, that's for sure."

I looked over at Cate beside me. "This is Scott's shop? Scott the hair-dresser?"

"Sure enough." My friend looked down at the huge, pink Swatch watch she wore on her left wrist. "We're right on time." She pushed open the silver door to the left of the window and held it open while I walked into the most amazing hair salon I'd ever seen. I couldn't figure out what to gawk at first – the beautiful wallpaper of giant dahlias in bright colors, the antique mirrors that hung in front of the two salon chairs, or the barnwood that clad the check-in desk. It was so wild and so eclectic that I didn't think I would ever get tired of being there.

Then, when a huge man with tattoos on every inch of visible skin, a massive nose ring, and a smile came to the desk to greet us, I was totally sold. I would get my hair cut here for the rest of my life. "I'm Harvey, and this is Cate. We're here for cuts. You must be Scott?"

Often, people assumed I was extroverted because I was really friendly, case in point here, but really, I just loved people. And I loved unusual people who were comfortable being themselves the most. Clearly, Scott was one of those people.

"Hi Harvey and Cate. Yes, I am Scott. Glad you came in. Harvey, Cate has insisted you go first. That okay with you?"

I looked at Cate who wiggled her eyebrows toward me, and then said, "Sure." Scott pointed toward the chair closest to the front of the shop and then said, "Let me get you a chair, Cate. We can all talk together." He then came around the desk and picked up a paisley velvet wingchair with one arm and brought it to his styling station.

I slid down into the styling chair, and as Scott pumped me to the height where all of my head appeared in the gold-filigreed mirror in front of me, he said, "So what are we doing with all this beautiful, curly wildness? Not coloring out your racing stripes I hope."

"I call them the same thing," I said, tugging at the white stripes of hair that were growing ever wider near my temples. "No, I actually like those. But color? I hadn't thought of that."

Cate winked at Scott and then looked at me. "That's actually Scott's specialty. Color, that is."

I turned my head and looked at Cate. "Oh, it is, is it?" I put my hand over my mouth and whispered very loudly. "You brought me here to fulfill your evil plans for purple haven't you?"

Scott tapped my shoulder. "I'm really hard of hearing, so if you could, please be sure I can see your lips in the mirror. That way, I can fill in what I miss by reading your lips."

"Oh, I'm sorry. I was just teasing Cate. She's been trying to get me to do a purple stripe in my hair for months now." I looked steadily into the mirror and spoke a little more slowly.

"Oh, I like the idea of a stripe," the stylist said as he pulled his fingers through my hair. "But I think blue, like a shade darker than royal, would be better."

I blushed and tried to picture it. But I was not a person who had been gifted with the ability to visualize things. Fortunately, I was very trusting, and Scott looked like someone I could trust. "I like the sound of that. That is my favorite color."

"I thought so," Scott said. "Now, let's get you washed up." He led me to the wash basin, which was delightfully covered in flower stickers. As he draped the towel around me, he said, "You probably already know this, but curly hair needs special care."

He stepped in front of me so he could see my mouth as I responded. "I know some, but I'd love to hear it from an expert." So while Scott gave my hair a great scrub and then almost put me to sleep with the most amazing head massage, he told me all about the schedule for washing my hair, what kind of towel I needed to dry it with, and what shampoos and conditioners he'd recommend.

When he was done, he led me back to the chair, and Cate waved a notebook at me. "Don't worry. I wrote it all down," she said. "You looked like you might not be able to pay attention at the moment."

"I would pay just to have someone wash my hair for an hour," I said with a contented sigh.

"You know, that might be a really legit line of business if someone can get the marketing right," Scott quipped. Then his expression got serious. "Thoughts on a cut."

"Honestly, I know I just met you, but I trust you. Do your thing."

Scott grinned. "I love when people say that."

For the next thirty minutes, I watched as wisps of hair fell to the ground and wondered exactly what the final product would look like, especially with the new blue stripe he was applying to the asymmetrical cut. I would have to wait, though.

While the dye set, Scott set to work on Cate's black tresses, and within twenty minutes she had this cute, sassy cut that fell across her forehead at the perfect angle to not block her vision for a moment.

We chatted as Scott worked, and I found out that he and his wife had recently moved to town. They had two children, ages four and six, and they were cat people. Maine Coone Cat people to be specific. The three of us spent a fair amount of time discussing how Maine Coones were really the ideal cat – robust enough to handle rugged handling like a dog, but cuddly, too. Plus, they were pretty independent, which we all agreed was both a strength and a major character flaw. But it was their cute chirp of a meow that had made us all fall in love. Scott even showed us pictures of his cat Moose on his phone. I knew I'd have to meet that cat someday.

As soon as I got back in the chair, Scott removed the foils and smiled. There it was, a bright blue stripe next to my white one. I loved it.

"So I'm guessing you're a pomade and go kind of woman," Scott said, "but I'd like to dry and style you today . . . no extra charge. That okay?"

I laughed. "Sure." Stylists always wanted to play with my hair. Something about how much of it I had and its curliness was irresistible to hair artists. "Just no flat irons, please. I always feel guilty when I can't maintain that for more than a few hours."

"I would not even try it. The humidity would just undo it as soon as you went out the door."

I nodded. "Yep." I had to admit being pampered felt pretty good. I felt my shoulders drop a millimeter as Scott fluffed and finger-curled my hair.

"So there was a murder yesterday, right? I didn't expect St. Marin's to be a place for murder."

So much for my relaxed shoulders. "You'd be surprised," I said.

"Yep. If Baltimore had murder rates like this, Laura Lippman wouldn't have to write fiction."

For a second, I watched Scott's face to see if our comments were worrying him. The guy had kids after all. But he seemed fine. Nonplussed, in fact. I loved that word.

"So who was the guy who was killed?"

"The local track coach," Cate said. "He coached at the high school but also trained individual runners. Our friend Mart was one of his athletes. She found him, actually."

Scott shivered. "Oh, that must have been awful."

"It was. She's my roommate. It was a hard day." I remembered Mart's frenzied face as she'd run into the shop.

I watched as Scott somehow managed to get the giant tsunami of a wave on the right-side of my head to curve perfectly against my face and sighed. I was going to have to come here all the time now. That was going to be a big blow to my budget for Lu's tacos.

"Police have any leads?" Scott asked as he unvelcroed my cape.

Cate glanced at me before saying, "Not that I've heard. Sheriff Tucker is good, though. He'll catch the killer."

"Sure hope so," the stylist said as he followed us to the front counter. "I don't like the idea of a murderer being loose in town. Too bad about the guy, though. I used to be an athlete myself. I was thinking of taking up running. I could have used a coach."

I studied Scott's broad shoulders and muscled arms. "I would have pegged you for more of a rugby player than a runner."

"Football actually. Tight end."

I nodded like I knew what that meant. At least I'd learned enough to recognize it as a position in the game. "Ah, yes. Coach Cagle was good, I hear, as a coach at least."

A flash of something – anger, confusion, frustration – went across Scott's face, but it was gone before he looked up to take my debit card. "Good coaches, really good ones are hard to find."

"I wouldn't really know, I guess. Not much of an athlete myself." I took my card back." Thanks, Scott. This is amazing. I'll be back for sure."

We left the shop, and I felt more stylish and playful than I had in a long time. Cate kept flipping her hair from side to side, so I expected she felt the same way. "He's good," I said.

"Yep, the best. I hear his shop in Minneapolis was the hot ticket."

"Ah, that's where he's from. I couldn't place the accent." Scott said "O" like it was two syllables . . . kind of like how I said "I."

"Well, I'm glad he's here now." I glanced down the street toward Daniel's shop. "Think he'll like it?"

"Of course he will, but even if he doesn't, it's your hair . . . and you like it, right?"

I reached up to lightly touch my head. "I do. A lot."

"That's all that matters." She gave me a hug and headed back to the co-op.

I unwrapped Mayhem's leash from the light pole where she'd waited patiently while her adoring fans showered her with dog treats – I could tell by her swollen belly – and we walked toward Daniel's shop.

5

I needn't have worried about my hair. Daniel complimented it, made a joke about the blue stripe – "Getting full sleeves of tattoos next, Ms. Beckett?" – and then began telling me all the details about the Volvo that had quit running at 120 miles. "Blown fuse, I think, but I have to take the entire back end apart and have a special tool to get at it . . ." I glazed over at that point and started thinking about those round fuses that I'd had in a couple of the apartments I'd lived in. That led me to think about the glass insulators that used to be on power lines and how Woody had dozens of them in his workshop. And that made me think about the drives my parents used to take when I was a kid and how I'd watch the power lines for miles.

Eventually, my train of thought wound back around to the runners we'd seen the day before. I didn't talk about it, but I had once trained for a marathon back when I lived in San Francisco. It was one of those run for charity things, and I'd been great at the raising money part. Not so great at the running. An injury had sidelined me for the full marathon, but I did complete the half. Mom had come to cheer me on, and she'd even bought a goofy hat – like the one I'd worn to support Mart – and made her way around the race points to cheer me on.

I must have started smiling at the memory because Daniel said, "Somehow, I don't think you're smiling about my ten-minute rundown on why I hate Volvos."

Shaking my head a bit, I said, "Oh, sorry. I got lost in my own thoughts. What were you saying?"

He kissed my cheek and said, "Never mind, my punk rock girl. I was just venting." He wiped his hands on a rag that he always kept in one pocket of his coveralls. "What were you thinking about?"

I stretched my arms high above my head. "Running."

"Coach Cagle?"

"Not specifically, but kind of." I told Daniel about the runner in the shop this morning and about how even the newest person in town had known about the murder.

"You're surprised. I expect Scott heard about it the minute he opened yesterday morning. I hear people like to gossip in hair salons." Daniel winked at me. The man had never set foot in a hair salon in his life. He did, however, have a very committed relationship with a little old white-haired man up on the way to Easton. The guy cut his hair every two weeks for just five dollars a cut. When that man died, Daniel was going to be devastated.

I shrugged. "I guess. I am just always surprised by how fast news travels here."

"Not much else going on in the off-season."

"Not much but fuses that blow at 120 miles."

Daniel laughed. "You were paying attention."

I leaned over and kissed his cheek. "Join us for an *Outlander* binge tonight. Mostly us girls, but you're more than welcome."

"You know I'd love to watch an attractive Scotsman woo my woman, but I think I'll pass." He kissed me softly on the lips. "See you tomorrow. I'll come by at lunch to get more done on the float."

I waved as Mayhem and I left. I started to say goodbye to Taco on his dog bed by Daniel's office, but since his feet were in the air, I figured the kindest goodbye was a silent one.

My route home took me right up Main Street, so I decided to stop in and see Elle, partially because I wanted some spinach and lettuce for a salad and partially because I thought I could snoop around about her new business plan. Fortunately, the business part was easy to suss out as she and Woody were talking about it at the front door when I walked up.

"Howdy, Stranger," Woody said as he gave me a firm handshake. I appreciated handshakes, more than I did hugs actually. There was something personal yet not too demanding about them.

"Hey Woody. Hey Elle. What you two doing?"

Woody looked to Elle and then back to me. "Actually, we were just talking about you."

I felt my face flush. "That bad, huh? My ears weren't burning." I wiggled my eyebrows because I never could wiggle my ears. "So why am I the big news?"

Elle spun me around so I was facing the shop, and I saw what she had created from all the lumber she'd been working with earlier – big planter boxes that were mounted to the front of her shop below the windows. "Want some?"

"Are you kidding? I'd love some. These are amazing. Elle, is this what you were making when I walked by before?"

She grinned. "It is. Woody gave me the specs, and I thought I'd try it out. This is the new part of my business." She glanced over at Woody. "Well, *our* business."

"You're making planter boxes as a business?" I asked, a bit puzzled. That seemed like a mighty specific item, especially on the scale of these boxes. They were almost four feet wide and two feet deep. Perfect for a storefront, but less so for a house.

"Well, yes, but other garden-related wood crafts, too. Our idea is that Woody could build – on site if necessary – and I could fill the items or provide the seeds for do-it-yourself folks." Elle was bouncing on the balls of her feet.

"Right. Planter boxes of all sizes, raised beds, even benches and such for landscaping. We're calling it 'Box and Bloom.'" Woody said with a smile. "What do you think?"

I was already imagining all the things I wanted them to create for our yard. Mart, Elle, Cate, and I had tackled garden boxes this spring, but now, I knew I needed some planters for the windows, maybe a bench or two for the side yard. I could even ask Elle to give me a plan for a perennial shade garden. "I love it," I said. "I'd like to order two planters for the shop for as soon as possible. I'll fill them with autumn flowers and then something for winter. You can guide me, right?" I winked at Elle.

"Absolutely. But you don't need to order them. We're going to build them for you for free, Harvey, if you'll let us. We'd just like to put a little sign in the boxes to advertise. What do you think?" Elle's cheeks were rosy around her big smile.

"Oh, I love that. Happy to advertise, and I'll ask Mrs. Dawson to do an ad for the newsletter, too, okay?"

Woody let out a small chuckle. "I'll leave you to the marketing. I have some planter boxes to build. Bring them by tomorrow, Harvey?"

"If you can build them that fast, sure."

"Oh, they're almost done." Woody waved as he headed out the door.

"He knew you'd say yes," Elle whispered as she turned back to her planters. "Your reputation for kindness proceeds you." She bent down and hefted a big bag of organic potting soil. "Want to help?"

"Absolutely." I tied Mayhem to another light pole, confident that with Elle's ever-present bowl of water for passing dogs and her adoring fans, the pup would be fine, and proceeded to spend the next hour planting whatever Elle handed me. By the time we were done, the planters looked amazing – all bright colors against burgundies and greens that set them off. Her shop had always been gorgeous, but now, it was even more so. "Oh, I can't wait to see what you do at my place."

"I'll come by tomorrow afternoon and get them filled, okay?"

"Perfect. Now, can I buy some lettuce and spinach . . . and maybe use your bathroom to wash my hands?"

A bag of baby spinach and a head of butter leaf lettuce in hand, Mayhem and I made it home with just enough time to prep a big salad and pop the shepherd's pie into the oven.

I'd premade the pie because I didn't want to have to do all the cooking that night, and I'd had a dedicated audience, even at eight a.m. While I'd browned the hamburger and boiled the potatoes, Aslan had sat on top of the refrigerator watching. She wasn't allowed on the counters, a lesson she learned from sheer terror when I'd placed sheets of slightly crumped aluminum foil on all the countertops to deter her, but she taunted me by going right from a bar stool to the fridge in one leap. Now, she was sitting there licking her paws as if she was a lioness watching her servant prepare her dinner.

I had rolled my eyes at Mayhem, who was pretending to be more nonchalant about the possibility of hamburger fat under the peninsula. Both of them were ridiculous, but I was glad Taco wasn't here. For a low, slow basset, he was might quick and mighty tall when he stood up on those back legs to grab something off the counter. Just last week, he'd consumed the entire batch of chocolate chip cookies Mart had made. It's a good thing he was on the portly side or all that chocolate might have been problematic.

Now, Aslan and Mayhem were sleeping back-to-back on the couch. It wasn't a position they took up casually – there was a lot of eying and pillow smooshing involved – but more and more, I thought they liked each other, even if they wanted to pretend they didn't. They weren't fooling me, though. I knew that as soon as that pie came out of the oven, they'd both be waiting patiently for Mart to give them a taste. She was a total sucker for their subterfuge.

As I pulled the pie out of the oven, I heard Mart's car pull into the driveway, and as she came in the door, I said, "Perfect timing!" and gestured toward the steaming pie, the crisp salad, and the two glasses of red wine.

"That looks so good," Mart said as she draped her long, hand-knitted scarf over the bar stool, washed her hands, then grabbed the spoon to serve herself a mashed-potato-heavy serving of pie. "Thank you."

"You're most welcome," I said as I slid in next to her. "I hope you like the wine." I was no sommelier but I had popped into Chez Cuisine, after calling ahead to be sure Max wasn't in, to ask

Symeon's advice on the proper pairing. He'd recommended a shiraz, and I was excited to see if I'd met Mart, the wine expert's, high standard.

She picked up her glass and gave it a swirl. Then, she took a deep breath with her nose in the glass and promptly put it down. "Needs to breath a bit more." She looked over and saw my crest-fallen expression. "No, it's a perfect choice. A medium-bodied shiraz, notes of plum. Just needs a little more air in it."

I nodded like I knew what any of that meant and filled my plate, following Mart's lead on the mashed potatoes. "How was the day?" I asked as I took a sip of my wine. I didn't think more air would change my opinion of the wine much.

"Well, I stopped by the high school track to do my run since they have the lights on for football practice, and you won't guess what I heard?"

"A long string of numbers and then 'Hut!'? A cheerleader asking if her basket fold was tight enough? A tuba?" I gave her a sly smile.

She tilted her head and smacked my hand. "Okay, yes, but also, two of the teachers at the high school had filed a sexual harassment lawsuit against Coach Cagle."

"Oh, wow. So I guess he wasn't just nasty to teenagers, then?"

"Apparently not." Mart finally took a sip of her wine and the smiled. "It's good. No, I heard a couple of the cross country runners talking. A math teacher and a guidance counselor had asked students to come forward if they'd been harassed. Apparently, they were putting together a big case with a lawyer from Annapolis and everything."

I chewed a bite of the salad and thanked the gods of balsamic for simple salad dressing that was so good. "But the case hasn't been heard yet?"

"I guess not. The girls were saying that the teachers and some students had gone to the principal and then the school board about it, but they hadn't taken action. So they decided to sue." Mart slipped Mayhem a big piece of hamburger. Total sucker. "I ran behind the girls for a few laps, so I got the whole scoop. Apparently, they were suing for millions."

"Wow. That's serious." I leaned back in my chair and stretched. "And why haven't we heard about it before? I mean, I couldn't wear new shoes without the entire town knowing. Something this big . . . it seems like it would slip out."

Mart slid a spoonful of potatoes up to Aslan's resumed spot on the fridge and acted like I could not see her. "Yeah, I thought about that, too. Maybe they signed non-disclosure agreements or something to protect the case."

That seemed reasonable. It would probably be more effective if the defense didn't know what people were going to say in the hearing. "Still, it's surprising. We are not a secret-keeping place. I mean everyone knew what a scuzzbucket he was. I'm just surprised no one knew."

Mart stopped mid-scoop of her second helping of pie. "Maybe someone did. Maybe someone killed him because they found out."

"Why would they do that before the case went to court? I mean, then justice wouldn't be served." But as soon as I said it, I knew the flaw in my thinking. "Unless . . . someone was sure he wouldn't get what they thought he deserved and decided to take matters into their own hands."

"I'm just saying," Mart said around a mouthful of peas and carrots. "What is it that Inspector Gamache is always saying?"

"What killed people was a feeling," I whispered.

6

M art and I watched six episodes of *Outlander*, and while I enjoyed the costumes and Jamie Fraser, I couldn't get what Mart had told me out of my head, even in the beautiful eighteenth century Scottish Highlands. What if someone had killed the coach because they were afraid the lawsuit wouldn't be enough? What if they decided it could never be enough?

I thought of the runner who had been in the shop, Tiffany Steinburg, and wondered if she had known about the lawsuit. I decided I'd give her a ring – she'd placed a special order for some running books with Marcus by phone yesterday – and suggest a couple more titles for her while also seeing if I could figure out whether she was part of the lawsuit. Elle had thought she sounded really angry, but angry enough to kill instead of just sue? That was the question.

As I showered, I planned out my question strategy. It wouldn't work for me to interrogate her of course, but I couldn't sound too offhand either. I had to have a reason for asking, something she could relate to.

I was spreading pomade in my hair when Mart propped her hip against the bathroom door. "So how are we sleuthing today?"

I tried to act naively befuddled, but Mart was on to me. "Don't even try it, Harvey. I could see the gears working behind your eyes all night last night, and now you're wearing the 'What's my angle?' face."

"I wasn't aware my face had angles any longer. It's softening into a warm roundness that I associate with kind women who bake cookies, and I kind of like it," I said testily.

"I like it, too. Middle age suits you. But seriously, I'm the one who found him, so if you're sleuthing, so am I."

I washed my hands and dried them on the towel by the door as I followed Mart into the living room. "Okay, so there's this woman—"

Just then, a sharp knock at the door was followed by the sound of the door opening and our alarm being shut off. Only one other person would come by this early, walk in without being invited, and proceed to make herself this much at home. My mother.

My parents had recently moved to St. Marin's from Baltimore to begin their retirement, and my mother was taking full advantage of her close proximity to try and build the kind of relationship she – and I – had always wished we'd had. The only trouble was that my mother kept forgetting that friends had boundaries.

"Well good morning. I figured you'd both be up and about, and I thought I'd see if I could walk with you to town, Harvey." Mom's voice was chipper, fresh, and totally clueless about her social faux pas. God love her.

"Sure, Mom, but it'll be a few minutes. I still need to eat some breakfast. Have a seat?" I gestured toward one of the bar stools in the kitchen, and Mom scooped up Aslan and began rubbing her chin as she leaned against the counter, right in front of the coffee pot.

I widened my eyes, gritted my teeth, and shot Mart a look that said, "Help me before I strangle my mother over coffee." Fortunately, Mart was fluent in my looks, as she'd already proven once today, and she guided my mom and Aslan around the peninsula to the aforementioned bar stool. "Good to see you, Ms. B. You're up early."

"Oh goodness," Mom said, "I've been up for hours. Already did a Zumba class and had a Zoom meeting for the Maritime Museum fundraiser." Then she looked from Mart to me. "I'm a morning person, but clearly, I am not amongst my compadres."

"We were up late watching *Outlander*," I groaned. "It's so addictive."

"I know," Mom said, getting even perkier. "That Jamie."

I laughed. "I won't tell Dad."

"Are you kidding? Your father has just as big a crush on Claire."

"Too much information. Too much information," I said and started the coffee grinder with the hopes of derailing this line of conversation. Fortunately, it worked because when I finished grinding the beans down to a powder that required two coffee filters to contain, Mom had moved on to other topics much less awkward and far more interesting than the Frasers.

"So you two heard about the murder at the high school, right?"

I grimaced. Despite her enthusiasm for sleuthing, Mart tensed at the mention of Coach Cagle. But she nodded. "I actually found his body," she said in a small voice.

"Oh, honey." Mom stood, put Aslan down, and wrapped Mart in a big hug. My best friend melted into my mom's embrace, and I saw some of her anxiety fade.

I smiled and then came around the counter to join in. Group hugs were some of the world's best inventions.

"Thanks, Mama Beckett. I needed that, but yeah, I'm okay. In fact," Mart glanced my way, clearly saw my frantic head shake, and plowed forward anyway, "Harvey and I were just talking about how she has an avenue to explore about the murder."

I sighed. Clearly, my best friend and my mother had similar thoughts about boundaries.

"You do, Harvey? Oh do tell. You know I love a good adventure, especially with my girl. My girls, I mean." She slid her arms around our shoulders. "Who are we interrogating today?"

BY THE TIME I'd had coffee and a bowl of cream of wheat, Mom and Mart had expanded on my plan to call Tiffany. Now, Mart was going to call her about helping her beef up the running section at the store before going on a run. "Runners are always looking for new running partners, especially if we do distance. She'll say yes." Then, we were going to go for dinner.

I groaned. Now dinner conversation would probably be about mileages and routes, times and running shoes. But we were going to a steak house with great margaritas, and Mom was coming, so there would be baked potatoes and someone to kick under the table when Tiffany and Mart started talking too long about pronation. I had long ago exhausted my interest in understanding which direction my feet rolled when I walked. The answer, for me, was always Birkenstocks.

Still, I was eager to get more information about what Tiffany knew and to see if her bond with Mart about running might get us closer to the killer. Plus, expanding our running section was a good side benefit. Woody had finished some new bookcases for us a few weeks back, and I was slowly filling them up with eye-catching titles that were great to face out. I couldn't yet afford to stock them with multiple copies of big sellers, but I didn't want the shelves to be empty, even if they were up above the main stock area.

By noon, Mart had the plans made. She and Tiffany were meeting at the store at three o'clock before they did a ten-mile run – "Just a short one today to try out how our paces work together," Mart said as my ankles began to hurt at just the thought – and then they would go to our house to shower and come back to the shop to meet Mom and me to talk books before dinner.

I made Mart promise to stop by and pick up Mayhem for protection before they went home. I didn't like the idea of her alone in our house with someone who might be a murderer. I didn't know that Tiffany was dangerous, but Elle had been unnerved by her tone – I wasn't taking chances. Tiffany didn't need to know that Mayhem was far better as a paperweight than an attack dog.

Sometime in the early afternoon, as I stood on the beautiful library ladders that Daniel had asked Woody to make for me to go with the new shelves facing out the gorgeous Penguin Classics versions of Amy Tan's books, I briefly entertained the idea that maybe I should tell Sheriff Mason what I knew. But then, I dismissed the idea because, well, I didn't really know anything. I couldn't very well share my knowledge when mostly I had the gossip of two teenagers and some harsh words overheard by someone else. He clearly would not be interested in that lack of information . . . at least that's what I told myself.

When Tiffany showed up in neon Lycra, I smiled. As much as I wanted to catch a killer and get them off the streets, I also hoped that Tiffany might turn out to be awesome just so she and Mart could share running. I did my best to listen and support Mart, but I really just didn't have that much to say about the beds of running shoes.

Tiffany had brought a list of the running books she'd found most helpful, and I promised to review them while she and Mart ran so that we could talk when they came back. Her list turned out to be great – some books on technique and some on mindset, a few titles for beginners and some for more advanced runners, too. By the time she and Mart stopped by about four forty-five to get Mayhem, I had already placed an order for a copy of each suggestion.

"Thanks for that list. I'll be glad to have more useful titles to suggest to the runners who stop in," I said as I handed her and Mart cold bottles of water. "See you guys soon."

"I cannot wait for some sour cream," Tiffany said with a wink at me as she held the door for Mart, and once again, I hoped she wasn't a killer. I liked a woman who appreciated sour cream.

Mayhem gave me a brief glance as she trotted out the door with the women as if to say, "They'd better not expect me to run home." I smiled. I was not making any promises.

At five, as planned, Mom showed up, looking every bit ready for a steak house with her pink cowboy boots and T-shirt that said, "Big Miss Steak" next to a picture of an animated steak carrying a purse. My mother never was one to disappoint.

A few minutes later, when Mart and Tiffany hadn't returned, I texted Mart but got no response. Assuming she was still in the shower, I suggested to Mom that we walk to our house and meet them. "We can take my car. Scooby-Roo needs a drive once in a while," I said.

The air was crisp, so we walked quickly down Main and over the couple of blocks toward our house. As we turned the final corner, I saw blue lights flashing and started to run. The police cruiser was at our house, and I just knew something terrible had happened.

A deputy put his arm across the door as I ran up. "I live here. Move," I shouted.

"Harvey Beckett, your manners, please," Mom said as she caught up. "Officer, this is my daughter's home. Could you please explain what is happening here?"

"Everything is okay, Harvey." I felt a surge of relief when Tuck's voice came from the hallway beside the front door. "It's okay, Officer."

The deputy gave me a sheepish shrug, and I tried not to glare at him as I passed. "What is going on, Tuck?"

"Someone broke in," Mart was sitting in the living room, her hair still wet from her shower. "I was just about to text you."

"Someone *may* have broken in," Tuck corrected. "A window from your backyard was broken, but it could have just been an accident."

"How does a window in our fenced backyard get broken by accident?"

Tuck grinned. "Baseball. You've got some pretty good sluggers in your neighborhood." Tuck regularly coached baseball for the little league teams, so he would know if we had kids in our neighborhood. I supposed that was a possibility, but since we'd lived here for almost a year and never even had as much as a stray frisbee in our yard, I doubted it.

"Really, Tuck? What's going on?" I grimaced. My voice sounded harsher than I intended.

Tiffany cleared her throat from my reading chair. "Oh, Tiffany.

I'm sorry. I forgot you were here." The woman looked frazzled, even in her sleek, high-waisted jeans and Boho shirt.

She smiled weakly and said, "I found the glass." I stared at her, not quite understanding.

"I told her to have a look around while I showered," Mart added. "So she saw the broken window before I did and called Tuck."

Tiffany stood and walked toward the window. "The glass was broken in. On the TV shows they always say that means someone was trying to break in, right?"

She looked at Tuck for confirmation. "Typically," he said quietly.

I looked at the usually confident sheriff but decided not to ask about his hesitation. He was still gathering information after all. "Any sign of what broke it? A baseball maybe?" I looked at the sheriff with a wry grin. We both knew this wasn't a baseball.

"No," he said. "It appears that whoever broke the window took whatever they used with them."

"Sheriff, over here." The young deputy from the front door was standing by the broken window. "Looks like blood."

"Oh, that's good, right?" I said hurrying over. "You can type it and run it through CODIS to find a match."

"Slow down there, Castle," Tuck said with a shake of his head. "You didn't touch the window, did you?" he asked turned toward Tiffany.

"No, of course not. Why would I touch the window?" Her voice was squeaky. "I didn't want to get cut, I mean."

I stared at the woman. She was clearly on edge, but then, it's possible she was just uneasy because of the police presence. Some people really didn't like cops.

"Okay. Did you see anything else?" Tuck took a step closer to Tiffany, and she tried to back away but bumped her calves against my chair.

"No, nothing. Just the glass." She dropped into the chair. "I guess I probably did look out, but if I saw anything, I didn't remember."

I looked over at Mart, and she shrugged. Clearly Tuck had some questions about Tiffany's story, and if he was leery, I was leery. Especially since he didn't even know about her conversation with Elle yet.

"Alright," Tuck said, turning back to Mart and me. "We'll finish up here and be in touch. If you want to go—"

Mom interrupted. "We were on our way out to dinner anyway. We'll leave you to it."

Tuck nodded. "I'll lock up, and you can pick up the key on your way home?" He held my gaze until I agreed.

Then, the four of us loaded into my truck and headed south. The steak didn't sound quite as good anymore, but it took a lot more than broken glass and a spot of blood to turn off my appetite completely.

BY THE TIME we reached the restaurant, Mom's steady determination to keep the evening fun and light – at least until we began to pry about a murder – had paid off. Mart and Tiffany were regaling us with a detailed account of their ten-mile run, and I was hoping my half-hearted "ohs" and "uh-huhs" were placed appropriately because I wasn't really paying attention. Instead, I was trying to figure out what that broken window was about. Had someone broken in? Or were they just sending a message? The latter didn't seem likely because a pile of broken glass didn't say much that was specific. But it seemed odd to break the glass in a six-by-eight-inch square of window that wasn't close to a door if you were trying to break in. I was stumped.

After I parked behind the saloon-themed restaurant, Mom nudged me hard with her shoulder as we walked into the steakhouse. "Get your head in this game, Harvey. You have a real chance at some answers with Tiffany. You can figure out the window stuff later."

My mother had always struck me as partially psychic, but I didn't always love it, like now, when I really wanted to focus on who had broken our window. I sighed, though, and nodded. She was right. This was probably the only chance we were going to get to figure out what Tiffany knew and what she thought of Coach Cagle. If she was possibly a suspect, I had to have my head on straight so I didn't tip her off.

The hostess seated us in a booth so wide that I had to slide three times to get to the other end of it and could only point to the menus at the end of the table. I spotted a bright pink margarita on the page facing me, and before anyone else even got their menus open, I said, "I'll take one of those. A big one."

"You got it," the young woman said with enthusiasm, even though I realized, just then, that maybe she wasn't the person who would take our orders. Still, she didn't hesitate when she asked, "Anyone else?"

"Do you do pitchers?" Mom asked.

The question "Everybody want salt?" got a round of nods, and the hostess headed off to order a pitcher of pink margaritas.

"Watermelon? Grapefruit? Strawberry? Raspberry? It's anybody's guess," Mart said. "I like a little mystery." She winked at me, and I smiled.

"Sorry. Guess I jumped the gun a little bit there?" I said.

Tiffany winced. "Actually, now that you say it, I think I heard a gunshot before the glass at your house broke."

"You what?!" Mart nearly shouted. "A gunshot? You think someone shot into our house? Why didn't you tell the sheriff that?"

Tiffany shook her head and squeezed her face with her hands. "I don't really know. I just wasn't sure, and I thought maybe I'd been wrong."

"Actually, that makes a lot of sense," I said. "I couldn't figure out why someone would break that particular window, but if they were shooting, well, then maybe what they were aiming at was through that particular pane of glass."

Mart tilted her head back and looked at the ceiling. "You mean who? Who they were aiming at?"

I sucked in my lower lip. "Yeah, I guess. I mean there's not much value in shooting into a house unless you're aiming at something."

"Unless you're trying to scare someone," Mom added as a different young woman walked up with the largest pitcher I'd ever seen full of the pinkest drink imaginable. "Put her down right here, ma'am. And thank you."

The server then placed four tall-stemmed salt-rimmed glasses with bowls as big as my fully-spread hand on the table. "I'll give you ladies a few minutes to get started on these and come back to get your orders soon, okay?"

I nodded, and as the young woman left, Mart said, "She smart. She knows that the more we drink, the more we'll eat."

"The more we'll drink, too," Tiffany added with a sly grin.

"Just half a glass for me. I'm driving," I said, regretting that the Eastern Shore didn't have a robust public transit system.

"Oh, I think we'll be here long enough for you to have a full glass, Harvey," Mart said.

I eyed the giant glass and decided that the worst that could happen was we would have to eat dessert and let Mom fill the whole thing. I took a long sip, smiled, and then remembered what we were talking about. "So were either of you in the room when the glass broke?"

Both Mart and Tiffany shook their heads. "I was in the shower," Mart said.

"And I didn't even hear the glass break. I was in the guest room drying my hair. I only remember the gunshot because I heard it just as I put the hair dryer down. I didn't think much of it because where I live, people shoot all the time. Target practice. And hunting season opens soon." Tiffany took a sip of her pink drink. "But when I saw the glass, I thought maybe . . ."

"So it must have been shot from a ways off. Otherwise it would have been much louder." Mom sipped her drink as she looked thoughtful.

I stared at my petite, charity board member of a mother. "Since when did you become so gun savvy?"

Mom smirked. "I've been going to the gun range with your father."

"What?! When did Dad start to shoot? You two – we move you out of the city . . . soon you'll have camo seat covers in your Navigator."

"Your dad is a little nervous about all your near-death experiences, beloved daughter. Cut him some slack. He just wants to protect you." Mom put her hand over mine.

I took a deep breath. I had been in a few close calls lately, but seriously, my father was an accountant, a corporate accountant.

He wouldn't even use a pen most of the time. "Too permanent," he said. I couldn't imagine him with a pistol. Still, there was something strangely sweet about my daddy wanting to protect me. I'd have to thank him the next time I saw him.

I squeezed Mom's hand. "We definitely have to tell Tuck. Someone shooting into our house is terrifying," I said and took another deep swig from my glass.

Just then, the waitress returned to take our order, and we realized we hadn't even looked at our menus yet. We all scrambled for a few seconds, but then, we got our steaks and potatoes ordered, and I added one of those big fried onions that they try to make look less deadly by fashioning it like a flower. I needed breading and grease, both to comfort myself and to help absorb all the tequila in my drink.

Mom steered the conversation away from a possible shooting once our food order was in. "Harvey, if you'll text Tuck, maybe we can leave all this worry about earlier to him and get back to girls' night."

I nodded and took out my phone. "Tiffany thinks she heard gunshot this afternoon. Could someone have shot out our window?"

His reply was almost instantaneous. "Where are you?"

"Steak Saloon."

"Good. Still processing at your place, but we should be gone by the time you get here. See you in the morning."

I felt my heart skip when I read that last message, but I remembered what Mom had said about focusing and put my phone in my back pocket.

The conversation had moved back to running, and Mart wound us right around to Coach Cagle. "You know, Coach was a total jerk, but he did know his stuff." She raised her glass to start a toast. "To Coach Cagle, the best running coach around. May he rest in peace."

I widened my eyes at my best friend because even for her big personality this was a little much. Still, I played along and clinked my glass against hers and then Mom's. But when I went to toast with Tiffany, I saw she was just staring into her half-empty glass. "You okay?" I asked.

She looked up at me, and I saw rage behind her eyes. "I'm not toasting that man," she spat. Then she looked at Mart. "I can't believe you think he was a good person." Her voice was full of tears.

Mart put her hand on Tiffany's arm. "Oh, don't mishear me. I thought he was repugnant as a person, but he was a good running coach. And while I'm not superstitious about talking ill of the dead, I don't wish death upon anyone, especially not murder. That's all I meant." She met Tiffany's stare. "I'm sorry if that hurt you."

Mom kicked me under the table as if to say, "Here we go."

"So you knew him, too?" Mom asked.

Tiffany took another sip of her drink. "Unfortunately, I did. He was my running coach back in Minneapolis before I moved here. He trained me for the Olympics."

"You ran in the Olympics?" I blurted.

Tiffany smiled at me. "Almost. I came in fourth in the trials for the ten-thousand meters, so I didn't get to go. I was close." Her expression soured. "It wasn't worth it though."

"What do you mean?" Mart asked.

I took a long pull on my drink as I watched Tiffany look at each of us before she spoke again.

"Coach Cagle sexually harassed me for years when he was my coach. I tolerated him because he was the best. Like you said," she glanced at Mart, "he was a great coach. But it took me forever to recover from his treatment of me." She let out of a long sigh. "And then, he shows up here, in St. Marin's, out of the blue."

"Wait. Did he follow you here?" I could feel my heart start to race the way it did any time I heard about a woman being stalked, and this sounded like stalking.

Tiffany nodded. "I left Minnesota five years ago and came here because I love the water and thought the quiet country roads would be great for running. I'm a freelance graphic designer, so I could go almost anywhere. But this place was beautiful, and I thought it was quiet and small enough that I could get away from him."

"He found you, though?" Mart's voice was very quiet.

"He did. He found my website, posed as a potential client, and said he wanted to send a check for his deposit on a new logo design." She ran her finger on the rim of her glass and then slipped a few grains of salt into her mouth. "I had been so careful, and one slip . . ."

Mom grabbed Tiffany's hand. "No, do not go there. This wasn't your slip. This was a man stalking you. You did nothing wrong. Nothing."

Tears welled in Tiffany's eyes. "Thank you. I know that in my head, but . . ."

I took a deep breath. "I know. Every woman I know has a story about a time a man did something inappropriate, and every one of us feels like we somehow brought it on. That's what our culture tells us – that we are the ones at fault. But we aren't. We never are when a man harasses us, abuses us, assaults us, or stalks us. It's always their fault. Always." My voice was strident, angry. I hated that this had happened to Tiffany, hated it fiercely for her and for all the women I knew. For myself, too.

Mart smiled gently at me and then turned back to Tiffany. "Harvey is right. This isn't your fault. What did you do when you found out he was here?"

A small smile broke across Tiffany's lips. "I egged his house."

"You go, girl," Mom said.

"And his car," Tiffany added.

"That is amazing," I said. "You didn't let him intimidate you."

"Nope, I didn't seek him out and did my best to avoid any place he might be. I never ran alone, and I made sure all private information about me was gone. I moved, too, got a new apartment in a new complex so he couldn't find me. I love my life here, and that man was not going to scare me away from it."

"Woot! Woot!" Mart shouted with a fist pump. "That deserves a refill." She poured more of the pink goodness into each of our glasses.

Tiffany frowned and reached out to take my hand as she gripped Mart's even tighter. "But you have to know, I didn't kill him. I might have thought about it a lot, but I didn't. You believe me?"

I looked at this woman across from me and thought of all the times men had harassed me – at work, on public buses, in the library, at clubs. I had never been stalked, but enough men had touched me without permission and done other heinous things to me that I could understand Tiffany's statement. But saying she wanted to but didn't wasn't a guarantee that she hadn't. Still, now was not the time, and for once, I was quite happy to let the police handle this one.

I squeezed Tiffany's hand and smiled. "Thanks for telling us," I said. "I'm so sorry that happened to you." I meant every word I said.

OUR STEAKS ARRIVED a few minutes later, and they looked amazing. The table got very quiet as we all tucked into our food. My ribeye was perfect – just pink at the center and so flavorful that I couldn't even think about adding steak sauce. The potato was fluffy and covered in sour cream and bacon, and my side salad had just the perfect amount of Caesar dressing and the perfect number of croutons. It was all delicious.

I was just finishing up this wonderful pumpkin bread pudding that I'd decided to splurge on when I realized I – and everyone else at our table – was far too tipsy to drive. I was hoping the dessert might sober me up, but even my fuzzy brain knew that wasn't going to happen before the restaurant closed. If I hadn't been tipsy, I might have been worried.

I glanced at Tiffany. Her temporary sorrow and anger at her memories of Coach Cagle had seemed to fade as our conversation moved on to more pressing subjects, like how much time we'd need to do our hair for the Harvest Parade. Mom had, apparently, already decided she was going to join us as Violet, complete with a dark wig, and she'd convinced Dad to come on as Shermie, which I told her I'd see when I believed. By the time our pitcher of margaritas was done, Tiffany had signed on as Sally, and I was really hoping she wasn't a killer.

The bill came, and only then did I begin to wonder how we were all going to get home. I thought about texting Daniel and asking for a lift, but the blessings of a small town came to fruition before I had a chance. From over the half-wall at my end of our booth, a familiar voice said, "The party over there looks fun." And then my friend Stephen and his husband, Walter, peeked over at us and smiled. "Maybe too much fun? Need a lift, girls?" Stephen asked.

I blushed, which was probably not noticeable given that even a single glass of wine brings the red to my cheeks. "Actually, would you mind?"

The men stood, and Walter said, "Not at all. We're ready if you are." Then, they came around and extended their arms to help us up, which was more necessary than I expected. Soon, the six of us were grouped by threes, Mom and me with Stephen holding us up and Walter guiding Tiffany and Mart out. We must have looked a sight, but I didn't care. That was the most fun I'd had in a while.

As we reached the parking lot, I leaned over to Stephen and asked, "How long did you know we were there?"

He pulled me close against his side. "Oh, we saw you when we came in, but you looked like you were having a blast and we didn't want to interrupt. It wasn't our choice to sit so close, but it was great to hear you laughing so much."

I smiled. "Thanks. And thanks for this, too." I swung my hand somewhere in the vicinity of the car I thought was his. He helped me into the back seat and got my mom settled in the front. Mart slid over next to me and Tiffany beside her. Then, the next thing I knew we were at our house, and Walter was getting Tiffany settled in the guest room.

"I texted Daniel. He'll be here at eight to get you to go pick up your car, and I let the restaurant know why it will be there overnight," Stephen said as he placed my plaid pajamas on the bed. I had a half-formed thought about how nice it was to have good enough friends that they not only drive you home when you can't drive yourself but they also have no hesitation about opening drawers until they find your favorite pajamas.

· · ·

THE NEXT MORNING, I woke from a dreamless sleep to my alarm playing Billy Ocean's "Get Out of My Dreams," and I smiled. Stephen had left just a bit of himself behind with his choice of radio station. He'd gone to that tiny bit of trouble to switch over my beep and let me wake to his favorite, eighties music. I decided that signaled a special kind of friend. After all, it takes someone special to torture you with terrible synthesizer.

I'd thought I'd be hungover, but given the empty tumbler by my bed and the ibuprofen bottle in the bathroom, I figured Stephen had made sure I had pain killers and water, and they must have made sure Mom, Tiffany, and Mart had the same pre-sleep dosing because all three women were bright-eyed and bushy-tailed with cups of coffee in hand. "I made a big pot of steel-cut oatmeal," Mart said. "I figured we probably all needed a little healthier option after our indulgence last night."

Tiffany smiled. "Thanks for last night. It's been a long time since I had good friends to just hang out with." She sighed. "Sorry to bring the night down, though."

I flipped my hand at her. "You didn't bring the night down. Not at all. We have to be able to count on each other, right? Thanks for trusting us with that part of your life."

Tiffany smiled. "Alright, but let me doctor this oatmeal my way." She gestured toward the pantry beside the refrigerator. "Do you mind?"

"Make yourself at home," Mart said, and she and I grabbed bar stools beside Mom and watched Tiffany go to work. She grabbed dried apricots and cranberries and then chopped those up with some walnuts. Then, she zested an orange before mixing every-thing into the oatmeal pot with a generous helping of maple syrup. When she ladled the oatmeal a few minutes later, our kitchen smelled like fall, and I was so hungry I was thinking about chewing off my fingers.

The oatmeal was phenomenal, and when I complimented her, she said, "It's nothing. Just easy and healthy. The least I can do when I had to sleep in your guest room all night."

"Our bed is your bed," Mart said.

"Does that apply to me and the couch?" Mom quipped as she slipped her purse on her shoulder and headed toward the door.

I rolled my eyes as I kissed her on the cheek and kept an eye on her as she walked to her car.

Mart slid her messenger bag onto her shoulder and said, "I'm off. The winery has a big fundraiser for after the parade." She stopped and looked back at us. "Actually, you two might want to come. It's for RAINN, the rape, assault, incest national network. I could use help serving if you want to make some extra cash."

I looked quickly at Tiffany, hoping Mart hadn't overstepped, but our new friend was beaming. "That sounds amazing. But I don't want to be paid. If you need to pay me, then just donate whatever I'd make to the RAINN."

"Same here. You'll get us the details?"

Mart beamed. "Definitely. Thanks. Okay, see ya later." She bounced out the door, and once again, I wondered how I'd ended up with such a perky best friend. Still, I loved her.

As Tiffany cleaned up, at her own insistence, I walked over to the boarded-up window by our dining room. Tuck and his team had cleaned up well, and the board was all that was left of the shot. Still, it was unnerving, and I was eager to hear what the sheriff would say when I saw him at the store later.

I walked Tiffany to her car and handed her a to-go mug full of coffee. "Get it back to me on Saturday when we ride over to the fundraiser. Mart will need to be there way early, so we might as well plan to go together. Sound okay?"

"Perfect," she said before climbing into her car and beeping as she pulled away.

I really liked that woman, but she definitely had a reason for wanting Coach Cagle dead, and a good one, too.

7

D aniel pulled up a few minutes later, and if the giant grin on his face was any indication, he was thoroughly loving that I'd had to be driven home last night. "So you had fun, huh?" I shook my head and started to lift Mayhem into the cab of his pick-up truck beside Taco. "Actually, mind if we take your truck?" Daniel asked. "I know you don't get to drive her much, so I thought we could give her some road time."

"I love that idea. Just let me get the keys. Come in. I'll get you some coffee, too." I smiled as I held the front door open behind me. Daniel had bought me this truck a while back, and I loved it. But last night, it had been too small for all of us, and he was right – I didn't get to drive her often enough. His plan was a good one.

I was just coming back from my room with the truck keys when Daniel shouted, "What happened here?" I came back into the living room and saw him staring at the back window. Only then did I realize I had forgotten to tell him about the broken window.

"Oh, right. That happened before we went out to dinner last night. Don't worry. Tuck is on it."

"What?! Why was Tuck here about a broken window?" Daniel's face was suddenly bright red.

All the memories of what might have happened here came rushing back, and the fun lift I'd gotten from the margaritas and the time with friends last night came crashing down. "Well, it, um, it may have been a gun shot."

"What are you talking about, Harvey?" Daniel took three long strides and was now standing right in front of me. "Clearly, I need to be brought up to speed."

I glanced at my watch. "You do. But can I do that on the road. Tuck is coming to the shop at nine, and I don't want to miss him." The sheriff's text had said he'd only have a few minutes, and I didn't want to miss my chance to hear what he had to say.

"The sheriff is coming to your store. Again." Daniel's voice was practically a groan.

"He's a friend, Daniel. He comes by all the time." I was being purposefully obtuse, and I knew it. But I really didn't want another lecture about how I needed to stay out of police investigations. Plus, I didn't want to see the worry on Daniel's face.

My boyfriend let out a loud sigh and flung his hands in the air. "Let's go. But I want to hear what the sheriff has to say, too, okay? Deal?"

"Deal."

On the ride back to the Steak Saloon, with Mayhem and Taco tucked into their custom-made dog crates in the bed, I gave Daniel all the details I had about the window and the possible shot that Tiffany heard. Then, I told him about Tiffany's history with Coach Cagle.

To his credit, Daniel honed right in on the most important part of what I said, that Tiffany had been stalked and that he couldn't imagine what that must have felt like. He was one of those rare men who, right from the get go, understood that a woman was always the victim in a matter of assault, no matter what she did. In fact, he loved to quote comedian Dick Gregory – "If I'm a woman and I'm walking down the street naked, you still don't have a right to rape me." – any time a victim was blamed for her assault because of what she wore or what she drank or what she said a few minutes earlier. Just another reason I loved this guy.

"But it does mean she had a really good reason to kill him," I said after Daniel had finished his rant about how awful men were.

"She does, but let's give her the benefit of the doubt, right? Besides, we aren't investigating the coach's murder." He gave me a significant look as he pulled up next to the car in the restaurant parking lot.

"We are not." I tried to sound convincing.

We got to the store shortly before nine, and I had just gotten the alarm off and the lights on when Tuck and Lu came in. I was surprised to see the sheriff's wife with him, but I was happy, too. Lu was a fun, vivacious woman who was the perfect pair for her husband's prankster personality. "Lu, good to see you. What brings you in?"

Tuck pulled out a chair for his wife, and she smoothed her denim dress under her and sat down. "I asked her to come," the sheriff said. "Thought you should hear from her yourself."

I sat down across from my friend, and she smiled softly. "Coach Cagle has been accused of several sexual assaults and at least two rapes. I've been working with some of his victims, encouraging them to press charges. But they were scared," Lu said.

I nodded. I knew that very few victims reported sexual assault and even fewer testified because of the low rate of conviction and because of the way the victims got tried publicly for what many considered "their part" in the crime. But when Lu said that only point five percent of attackers ever went to prison for their crimes, I was stunned.

Tuck shook his head. "I try. But there's only so much I can do."

I rubbed my hands together and let out a long slow breath. "When you say that, it makes me understand why someone thought killing Coach Cagle was the right thing to do." I looked from Lu and Tuck, worried that I might have just offended them. After all, law enforcement was their life.

"You won't hear me arguing," Tuck said. "Now, I didn't say it was right, but I do understand why someone might do it. Still, we don't really know that's the motive."

Lu stared at her husband and said, "We don't *know* know, I agree. But we *know*." Tuck nodded.

I figured this might be the time to tell them about Tiffany, even though I felt a little like a rat sharing her story. Still, I knew that Tuck and Lu wouldn't go spreading gossip, and I also knew that Tuck needed to know, just in case my gut instinct was wrong. So I relayed what Tiffany had told us last night, and Tuck took notes.

"So that's where you all were going?" Tuck said with a shake of his head. "I told you not to get involved in this, Harvey.

"I know. But I didn't really know anything to share until last night, and here I am telling you." I raised my eyebrows innocently.

"You could have told me last night." Tuck's voice was stern.

"Actually, I couldn't. We had a few too many margaritas. Stephen and Walter had to bring us home."

Lu threw back her head and laughed. "That is great, Harvey. You deserve to kick back sometimes. And this information about Tiffany, it's good for the case." She leaned forward and held my gaze. "But I'm more worried about her." She reached into the pocket of her dress and pulled out a small blue card. "If the time seems right, maybe you can give her this."

I looked at the card and saw a number for RAINN's sexual assault hotline. "Sure. I don't know if she'd call, but maybe." I looked at the card again. "Got any more? I'd like to put a stack by the bulletin board in the café. You never know."

"Nope, you never do," Lu said. "I'll bring some by later today." She and Tuck stood. "You know there's a big fundraiser for RAINN at the winery on Saturday, right?"

"Actually, Tiffany and I will be working there with Mart. She just recruited us this morning."

"Great," Lu said. "Maybe you can introduce us? I'm always eager to meet new folks, but also, maybe . . ."

"Absolutely. Always good to know of people who can help. Thanks, Lu." I gave her a tight hug and then looked at the clock above the café counter. "Oh, man, Rocky will be here shortly."

"Got it. We'll bounce," Tuck said, and his wife winced.

"Nope. Doesn't work for you. Besides, I don't think anyone even says, 'Let's bounce' anymore," Lu said with a laugh. "See you Harvey."

For a Thursday, we were remarkably busy. Apparently, a lot of people from Baltimore and even Philadelphia had decided to spend the weekend in town for the Harvest Festival, so our foot traffic was up. We were selling pumpkin-themed books left and right, which I took to be a sure sign that those of us who love pumpkin outweighed those people on social media who seem to loathe the stuff. I, however, was finally wise enough to know not to engage that, or any debate, online and just reveled in the good sales figures.

Marcus's after-school entourage came in right on schedule. This bevy of teenage girls clearly had a crush on my assistant manager, and while he was obviously quite devoted to Rocky, he was also kind and polite to these young women. And his kindness meant they came back often, which I didn't mind. Bookstores aren't always the hang-outs for teenagers, but I liked their presence. Plus, they bought any book Marcus recommended. Today, he was telling them about *Artemis Fowl* and suggesting that while they were certainly too mature to be the intended audience, "I think you'll still enjoy the playful way Colfer uses the stereotypes about fairies and such."

The girls were agog with his kind assessment of their literary abilities, and I was equally impressed at his ability to recognize books that might not seem a good fit for a reader but actually were perfect. These teens loved urban fantasy, so steering them to a middle grade series that featured character types they'd know, but a in a new way, was super wise and might just broaden their reading tastes a bit. Masterful, that guy.

I was just listening into Marcus's conversation with the girls as they checked out when Scott came in. I smiled as I saw my new hairdresser and hoped I had done his cut justice with my very slim efforts toward styling this morning. "Hey, Scott. Glad to see you here."

"Well, I had to return the favor of business for my new client and fellow business owner. Point me to the manga, please."

I nodded and walked him toward the small section of graphic

novels, comic books, and manga. "We don't have a lot here, so if you have recommendations of must-have titles, do let me know. I don't read much manga, but I'm always open to suggestions." I ran my hands through my hair, pulling on the blue stripe self-consciously. "In fact, the only graphic novel I've read ever was *The Watchmen*."

"Well, if you're only going to read one, that's a good choice. What did you think?" he asked as he pulled a Sailor Moon anthology off the shelf.

"I liked it. I mean I liked the characters and the plot, but to be honest, reading and studying pictures at the same time isn't my favorite. Probably I'd get better at it if I tried, but well," I gestured around the store, "with so much . . . I do love reading . . ."

"Got it. Too many books, too little time."

"Exactly." I looked back toward the front of the store to see a customer headed toward the register. "Well, just let me know if you need anything."

He nodded and turned his attention back to the shelves in front of him as I scurried up to ring up a customer's beautiful coffee table book of Andy Goldsworthy's art. I spent a bit of time talking to the older man about his purchase, and it turned out we were both avid Goldsworthy fans. By the time I thought to check on Scott, he was already in the café chatting with Rocky.

Marcus was tidying the front tables, so I took a minute to step over for my afternoon latte. As I walked over, I heard Scott say, "Oh yeah, I used to be fast – 4.6 in the 40-yard dash, if you can believe it." He patted the slim curve of his belly. "No way I could do that now."

"4.6 – that's fast. Like almost Olympics fast," Rocky said. "I never did have speed, just distance."

"You were a distance runner, Rocky?" I asked, totally butting in and not caring. "I didn't know that."

"I am a woman of mystery, Harvey Beckett. You should know that by now." She laughed. "Scott was just telling me that running was the best part of football for him."

"I don't think I've ever heard someone say that about football. After all, running doesn't have much to do with the ball, does it?" I shrugged.

Rocky and Scott shot each other significant looks. "Gracious, Harvey. Have you ever watched football?"

I felt my face redden. "Of course. But isn't the point to throw the ball and catch it?" As soon as the words left my mouth, I imagined a field with a bunch of men running – running very fast in fact – to catch the ball.

"And who catches--" Rocky started, but I interrupted her with a raised hand.

"Those fast dudes who catch the ball – you were one of those, right? Tight end?"

Scott chuckled. "Good memory. Yep, I was one of those fast dudes."

I smiled as I felt my brain trying to tick off some box. I needed a moment for my mind to catch up. "Well, I will not be moving at all if I don't get some caffeine. Fill me up, Rocky?" I held out my blue, hand-thrown mug.

"Sure thing," Rocky said as she winked at me.

As I watched her fill my cup, I tried to follow the gossamer thread of thought my brain was trying to weave. Something about Scott and running . . . I came back to the moment when

Rocky waved the cup of cinnamon-covered warmth beneath my nose.

"Earth to Harvey," she said. "You okay?"

I laughed nervously as I glanced from her to Scott. "Sorry. Just got lost in my thoughts there. Thanks for this." I waved to her and Scott and headed back to the bookstore. I just couldn't quite get to what my brain was saying, but I knew myself. It would all come together eventually if I just gave myself enough time.

Unfortunately, time was not something I had a lot of for the rest of the day. The customers kept coming in steadily, so I stayed on past my scheduled hours to help Marcus and to replenish our pumpkin books in the window. It just wouldn't do to have an empty window display before the weekend.

By the time we closed at seven, I was beat and really just wanted to go home, eat marshmallow cereal for dinner, and watch more *Outlander*. But we had a float meeting first, and we needed to get going on finishing our float. I didn't want to be here until midnight tomorrow trying to get everything finished.

Fortunately, Cate and Lucas came with Sasquatch, their Miniature Schnauzer, and, as usual, they had dinner in hand. This time, it was a huge platter of lasagna that Lucas had made from scratch and a large salad. Plus, I was thrilled to see a big box of his famous cupcakes. And soon we were joined by Stephen and Walter, our friends Henri and Bear Johnson, Pickle and Lois Herring, and even Woody, with my planter boxes at the ready. Mart brought Tiffany, too, and Daniel sauntered in with Taco just as we got everything set up.

The dogs gobbled down the special meal of chicken and rice that Lucas had whipped up just for them, and Mayhem then led their retreat to the dog bed in the window, where I saw both tourists and locals stopping to wave and take pictures. Once again, I gave thanks for my idea of having a dog-friendly shop. It probably was the primary source of my business some days.

Soon, everyone had paper plates full of pasta, crisp salad, and a cupcake (or two in my case), and we were perched around on the chairs and ottomans that Marcus and I had gathered in the fiction section. I again wondered about having some evening picnic-style potlucks here in the winter months – this kind of gathering was just so much fun, and when the tourist season pretty much shuttered after this weekend, maybe local folks would enjoy a quiet evening out at the bookstore. I texted myself to remember to look at the calendar for November and see if we could get that scheduled. Then, I focused all my attention on Lucas's amazing lasagna – with sausage and hamburger, perfect amounts of cheese, and a tomato sauce that was just the right amount of sweet and basil-filled. If I hadn't already had the second cupcake at the ready, I might have had seconds.

As we ate, we chatted about the harvest festival and the parade, about the latest news from the museum that Lucas directed, and, of course, about the murder. Mart and I exchanged a look when Henri mentioned the lawsuit, and I saw Mart reach over and discreetly rub Tiffany's arm. But neither of us said anything about what she'd told us. That was her story to tell, well, unless she was a murderer. But I was still hoping that wasn't the case.

Eventually, I figured we needed to get moving on the float, even though what I really wanted to do was rest my shoulders against Daniel's chest and talk with my friends all night, so I stood and put on my jacket. Soon, everyone followed suit, and we trudged out the back door of the shop into the cold, dark October night. Woody had brought by some workshop lights, so we could see back in the alley, and soon enough, we were hard at work hanging streamers, painting signs on pieces of old paneling that Daniel had pried from the back of his office wall, and figuring out how to secure a big, but very lightweight pumpkin, to a hay trailer.

PIckle and Bear were in a full-on debate about pumpkin lashing when Symeon stepped out from the back door of Chez Cuisine. He looked flustered, but I didn't think much of it given that he worked for Max. If I worked for that man, I'd be flustered – and irate – most every minute. But as I hung streamers from the gooseneck of the trailer, I saw Symeon's pacing behind the restaurant get more emphatic, and soon I heard him talking to himself, as if he was psyching himself up for something.

I caught Mart's eye and pointed toward Symeon with my head. She followed my gaze and then nodded before heading his way. They talked for a few minutes, and then, just as I finished making a total mess of my twist of yellow and orange streamers, they headed back toward us. "Hey, Symeon," I said as I lowered myself from the trailer. "You okay? Looked like you were working through something major over there? Max getting to you?" I tried to look sympathetic and not nosy, even though I felt completely nosy.

He looked at me with confusion and then smiled. "Oh, no, not Max. I can handle Max." He winked at me, but then his face grew dark again. "No, it's what I was hearing from one of my tables. My uncle . . ." He looked at Mart and then at everyone else, who had since stopped work to look at him. "Never mind. I don't want to gossip."

Tiffany stepped forward to the edge of the trailer from where she had been helping Daniel secure a custom-made dog bed as Taco's perch for the parade. "No, what did you hear? I want to know." Her voice was hard and brittle.

Symeon looked from Tiffany to Mart. When she shook her head slightly, he said, "It's nothing really. Just people talking, probably."

I felt a thud beside me, and then Tiffany was in Symeon's face. "Tell. Me. What. You. Heard," she said and thrust a finger in Symeon's face.

Symeon took a quick step back, and Henri stepped up and slid an arm around Tiffany's waist. "Clearly you have some feelings about Coach Cagle," Henri said calmly, " but there's no need to take that out on Symeon here. Surely you can see he's having a hard night?"

Tiffany's scowl slowly softened, and it seemed like she might be seeing Symeon for the first time. "Sorry," she said. "It's just, that man."

Hands raised, Symeon said, "You'll get no argument from me. He was a total cretin. I never liked the guy, but I didn't know he was that bad." He laced his fingers behind his head and looked up at the sky before turning back to Tiffany. "But maybe he was."

"Sorry," Tiffany said as she laid the hammer she'd been using on the trailer. "I think I'd better go." She hugged first Mart and then me and put an arm on Henri's shoulder. "Thanks, everyone. See you at the parade."

I watched her slip back into the shop and followed her, but by the time I reached the counter, she was already going out the front door. I turned the lock and watched her as she got into her car and sped off down the street. I felt the RAINN card that Lu had given me in my pocket and decided that tomorrow I'd find a way to see Tiffany and get that to her. Clearly, she had some unresolved struggles, and their volunteers just might be able to help.

8

F riday morning came too soon, but when my alarm went off, I was up like a shot. I had so much to do to prepare the store for the Harvest Festival. The Main Street Fair, which kicked off the festival, began at four p.m., and I wanted to be sure we had plenty of goodies – including some of our infamous "Book Grab Bags" for the kids. Each grab bag was going to include a coloring book, a chapter book, and a coupon for ten percent off their next purchase in the store. I'd ordered a whole bunch of fun but inexpensive titles a few weeks back, and my morning's work was to fill the pumpkin-shaped bags and have them ready for the Fair.

Plus, I wanted to beef up the pumpkin window display, change out the other window to focus on Autumn-themed fiction, including several copies of Isabelle Allende's *House of Spirits*, which Marcus's mom had just recommended glowingly in our latest newsletter. I'd also printed up a poster-sized copy of that newsletter with a "Sign-Up Inside" bubble attached in the hopes that we'd grow our mailing list over the weekend. This was our last chance to really grab the readers before the town got sleepy quiet for the winter season. I was hoping that more email subscribers might mean more special orders, especially if we offered discounted shipping for larger orders.

So I threw some bread with extra sharp cheddar under the oven's broiler as I double-checked that my backpack had everything I needed for the day. Then I ate as Mayhem and I walked to the store. I loved days like these – busy and full of potential, but they also made my stomach ache. I fed most of the cheese toast to Mayhem.

Marcus came in early that day, and so he staffed the store while I worked on the displays. When I was done, the windows were full and looked perfectly autumnal. I'd placed candles with artificial flames on pedestals and stools of various heights in both windows to tie them together. Then, I'd perched the books for each theme on ladders and chairs in the displays, leaving plenty of room for Mayhem's dog bed in the fiction window. Then, I'd placed small pumpkins and gourds from Elle's farm around in groupings and finally centered my newsletter poster and a sign that Cate had hand-painted from the leftover paneling last night that read, "All Things Pumpkin" to the left-side of the other window.

Outside, Woody had hung my new planters, and Elle was there filling them with the most amazing plants, mums and coleus with lots of bright yellow pansies in the front. The boxes were just the perfect touch, and I even loved the little card advertising the planters for sale in the corner below the fiction display. I had no doubt Elle and Woody would be getting lots of orders soon.

About noon, Galen walked in with Mack. The Bulldog headed right to the front window to join Mayhem and Taco. Galen picked up a couple of thrillers, including a copy of *The Summer House* by James Patterson. "How does this man write so many books?" he asked as I handed him his purchases.

"Help," I said. "He writes most of his new books with ghost-writers now, but he picks good ones, ones who get his style. And he has this whole new series of kids' books that are so fun." I pointed over to a cardboard display that Patterson's publisher had sent over for the holiday sales season. "He's got a good thing going, and he's good at helping other writers, too. I like him."

Galen smiled and snapped a picture of the display. "I like him, too. His books are so fun. Next time, I want a couple of those children's books, okay? Remind me? "

I smiled and then gestured to the front window. "Feel like leaving Mack for a while?"

"How could I tear him away?" He looked at the chubby English Bulldog. "I mean, literally. I can't carry him, and it certainly doesn't look like he's going to leave of his own volition. You don't mind?"

"Not a bit. Just come by before the fair starts and pick him up? I don't think I can hold all three of them back when the funnel cake stand arrives," I didn't know if I could hold myself back, now that I thought about it.

"See you then." Galen headed out the door and greeted Cate, who was standing with Sasquatch in her arms and pointing to the sleeping trio.

I stepped out the door. "Leave him. They can take a group nap."

"Perfect. I am running late and didn't know how I was going to drop him with Lucas at the museum and get my exhibition done by the time the fair started. You're a life-saver." She passed me the pooch and took off down the street at a brisk clip.

When I set Sasquatch in the window, he sniffed, turned a circle like a cat, and dropped onto his side like he was dead. Soon, I could hear four dogs snoring from the window, and I found myself a little jealous. Some days a group nap sounded like just about the best thing. All my friends and a good snooze – that would be so comforting. But not today, there was too much to do.

As Marcus and I bustled about filling gaps on the front tables, pulling down some overstock from Woody's new bookshelves, and adding everything from the backroom to the floor, I caught glimpses of lots of people photographing the puppy puddle in the front window. About every third person then came in to see the pooches in person and many of those folks bought books. Once again, hound-dog laziness was good for business.

About three o'clock, Marcus came back from his late lunch, and I decided to grab a quick snack and catch my breath in the café. Rocky brought me her newest café addition – a salted caramel, chocolate chip scone – and I dug in with my feet propped on a chair across from me. I leaned my head against the window.

The next thing I knew, the chair under my feet was jerked away, and I woke up to see Tuck smirking at me. "A bit tired, Ms. Beckett?"

I groaned. "I guess so." I sat up straight and hoped I hadn't been asleep long enough to flatten my hair on one side. It was a hazard of short, coarse, curly hair – it took on the shape of whatever it touched. Headbands left impressions that could be seen for days. "What's up, Sheriff?"

Tuck sat down in the chair he'd just removed and sighed. "Mart coming in today?"

I looked at the watch over Rocky's register. "Yeah. In fact, she should be in soon. Why?"

"Just need to ask her about Tiffany Steinberg." He pulled his hand down his face. "This is probably the worst time to need to solve a murder."

I raised my eyebrows. "Is there a good time?"

The sheriff smiled. "No. But with the festival, I have crowd control to do, and there's always a need to ticket the people who think it's okay to park in front of driveways. That stuff alone more than taxes my tiny staff of two." He let out another hard sigh.

A tinkle of the bell above the front door drew my attention, and I looked over to see Mart bouncing in as she laughed and pointed at the dogs. "Harvey, seriously, you have to see this."

Tuck and I stood up and headed toward the front door. There we saw a perfect circle of puppy-pillow prowess. Taco had his head on Mayhem's back. She had her head on Mack's back, Mack's head was on Sasquatch, and Sasquatch closed the loop by sleeping on Taco. We could not have possibly posed them that well if we'd tried.

I cooed and took out my phone. This was the stuff of Instagram gold.

After admiring the puppies, Tuck asked if Mart had a few minutes, and she nodded. "Mind if we use the backroom, Harvey?" Tuck asked.

"Sure as long as you don't mind me coming in and out. I need to set up the grab bags and all the supplies are in there," I said. I was being truthful. I did need to set up, and the supplies were there. But it could have waited. My curiosity just knew no bounds.

Mart and Tuck settled around the table in the back corner, and I busied myself by filling the goodie bags on the boxes out of which I took the supplies. My nosiness made my job far harder than it would have been if I had just taken the supplies to the tables Marcus had set up by the front door, but I couldn't bring myself to miss anything.

"Do you know where in Minnesota Tiffany was from, Mart?" Tuck asked, his pen poised over his notebook.

"Nope. But she could have told me. The only place I know in Minnesota is Minneapolis-St. Paul. Actually, that might be two places, right? If she'd named a town, I might not remember." Mart played with her pony tail for a minute. "She did mention running on the prairies, though, said the scenery around here reminded her of the lakes and long fields she used to train in. So maybe she was from some place rural?"

Tuck nodded. "And did she tell you how she met Cagle?"

Mart shook her head. "Nope. She just said that he had coached her for the Olympics. But she didn't tell me how she'd met him."

"She ran in the Olympics?" Tuck was writing quickly.

"No, she came in fourth at the trials." Mart stole a glance at me and winked while Tuck was focused on his notes.

I blushed. Of course, she would know I was eavesdropping. Chagrined, I picked up my now-full bags and headed out the door.

A FEW MINUTES LATER, Mart and Tuck emerged from the back-room, and he waved as he headed toward the front door. "Tuck get everything he needed?" I asked as casually as possible when Mart came to help me finish laying out the goodie bags.

"You are no end of nosy, woman," Mart said with a chuckle and then a sigh. "But no, I don't think I helped much at all. I just didn't have enough specific information." She organized the last row of bags, and we headed toward the table on the other side of the door.

As I straightened copies of our newsletter, I said, "What was he trying to find out?"

Mart lowered her voice. "Apparently, Tiffany Steinberg doesn't have any record in Minnesota. He couldn't even find a driver's license or anything."

I studied the stack of business cards in my hand. "Well, that probably makes sense, right? I mean, if she was trying to hide, she probably needed to change her name, right? It would be too easy to Google her actual name and find her, wouldn't it?"

"That's what I said." Mart straightened the vase full of Elle's flowers. "He agreed, but he did wonder if she'd given any hints about her life there." She dropped her voice a few more decibels. "It sounds like he really thinks she might be a suspect."

I felt a weight drop in my chest. "I was afraid of that." I looked at Mart. "I really like her, though, you know? I hope she didn't do this."

"Me, too," Mart said as she gave me a hug. "Me, too."

JUST BEFORE THE fair was officially set to begin, I ducked into the bathroom and did what I could with my face and hair. "What I could" amounted to a fresh application of powder, a little lip gloss, and a twist of the blue stripe in my hair to show it off. As I gave the curl one last tug, a thought came to mind, and I grabbed my phone as I headed toward the front tables to greet the already-growing influx of customers. I had just enough time to send off a quick text before the full-on meet-and-greet began.

The next two and a half hours flew by. We had customers the entire time, many of whom were just excited to meet the dogs and a few of whom also shopped.

Galen had come back for Mack at four fifteen, but then, he'd decided to stay. Soon, it began apparent he was also a huge draw, and Marcus had gotten him a table from the café. He was now signing autographs and letting people pet Mack. Clearly, he needed to write a book. He'd be an instant hit.

By the time seven p.m. rolled around, I was pooped, and we still had the parade the next day with prep for that to finish up. As soon as we finished clean-up, Rocky and Marcus headed out for a quiet night of movies and pizza, they said, and I found myself quite jealous. Still, my friends were coming soon, and rumor had it – via Stephen – that onion rings were on their way. I could eat the crap out of a hamburger and some onion rings, I decided.

Within a few minutes, everyone was gathered on the float at the back of the store, and we were munching on some of the best greasy food I'd ever consumed. Apparently, Walter had picked it up from a little counter-service place down in Princess Anne when he was on his way home with the pièce de résistance for the float: a full-size Woodstock costume that he'd had custom-fitted for Mayhem. I could have hugged him for the outfit, but mostly I hugged him for the onion rings.

Cate's pumpkin was perfect, and she'd brought a palette of paints to add some dimension to the coloring. Daniel was getting Mart's help with his bald cap. Walter and Stephen had decided that they were going to join the float as Linus and his blanket and were working on exactly how to drape Stephen in a blue blanket that would make it look like Walter was holding him. Just watching them try to figure that out was a huge boost to my energy. Then, when I saw Tiffany appear at the end of the alley in a giant yellow wig that made her look exactly like Sally, I knew the float was going to be perfect. Ridiculous but perfect, too.

We were almost done with our float work when I saw Scott come down the alley with people who I assumed were his family – a gorgeous woman in a long skirt and high boots and two children with amazing haircuts. "Oh, I'm so glad you could make it," I said as I walked over to shake his hand. Scott introduced me to his family, and the kids moved instantly toward Taco and Mayhem.

"I wasn't sure exactly what I was in store for when your text said, 'Meet us in the alley at eight,' but a chance for a little adventure sounded pretty perfect," Scott said.

It had occurred to me that one way we could figure out more about Tiffany was to introduce her to another person with Minnesota roots. Plus, I was still trying to figure out what exactly was nagging me about Scott. "So glad you guys could come. Let me introduce you around."

We made our way through the group with me telling everyone that Scott was the genius behind my new haircut, and everyone complimenting him and then saying they'd be in touch to get their own haircuts soon. When we reached Tiffany, I said, "You guys have something in common, actually. You are both from Minnesota."

Tiffany scowled for a second, but then, she put on a smile and reached out to shake Scott's hand. "Nice to meet you. You're the hair genius?"

Scott grinned. "I wouldn't go that far. But yes, I'm a stylist."

"I'll have to stop in." She tugged on her long, straight hair. "Clearly, I could use a cut."

"Here's my card. Just give me a call, " Scott said.

"Where in Minnesota did you say you're from, Scott?" I asked, trying to get to the information Tuck wanted.

"I lived most of time just outside St. Paul. Little town no one has ever heard of called Hastings," he said as he waved to his daughter who was infatuated with Taco's ears.

I looked over in time to see Tiffany blanch and then grab the float. "You're from Hastings?" she stammered.

"Yep, born and raised. You?"

"Um, from close to there. Nice to meet you." She looked at me, and her eyes were huge. "See you in the morning, Harvey." She tossed her wig up onto the float and almost ran down the alley.

Scott looked after her and then at me. "She okay?"

"Oh yeah, I think so. Been a long week, I think."

Scott furrowed his brow as he watched Tiffany's back recede down the alley. "Yeah, I guess so."

9

The next morning, I was at the shop at seven a.m. Daniel was due at seven fifteen with his friend who had a big enough truck to pull the trailer with all of us on it. That was something I hadn't thought of, so I was glad Daniel was on top of all things mechanical. If I had been left to my own devices, we would have been pushing the float down Main Street.

By eight, we had the float attached to the trailer, and Daniel had even convinced his friend to tie a stuffed Snoopy plush to his truck like a hood ornament. The parade began at nine, and so now all we had to do was wait and eat cinnamon rolls. I could do that easily, especially when Rocky handed me a huge latte sprinkled with cinnamon and sugar crystals.

"Oh man, this is gorgeous." I looked over. "Is that Woodstock in my foam?"

"Yep. I've been practicing. Peanuts-themed lattes all day. I can do Charlie Brown and Snoopy, too." Rocky was practically beaming. "I figured it might bring people in."

"Definitely. Now I want two more, one Charlie and one Snoopy please." I laughed. "That's such a good idea. Maybe you can teach me your foam tricks sometime?"

Rocky squinted at me. "A magician does not reveal her secrets.

I ROLLED MY EYES. "SO NOTED," I said with a laugh. "But seriously, I do need two more, one for Mart and one for Tiffany." I pointed toward the door at the two women who were just coming in. "Look at these," I waved them over.

"Holy cow! That's amazing," Mart said.

"It is," Tiffany added just before she took a sip. "But no foam Snoopy is keeping me from my caffeine."

"Alright, I guess we need to go get our costumes on," Mart said as she held up a tote. "Mind if we use the backroom?"

"Make yourselves at home. I can't wait to see."

Tiffany pointed from my head to my toes. "When are you going to put on your outfit?" She grinned at me.

"Fortunately, Peppermint Patty's outfit and mine are pretty similar. I'm all set." I looked down at my bright green T-shirt, black shorts, and sandals. "I just hope it doesn't get much colder or I'll need to put socks on under these puppies." I held one foot in the air to show my Birkenstock sandal. "That won't be pretty."

Rocky laughed. "You're right about that." She grabbed a piece of poster board with sketches of Snoopy, Charlie Brown, and Woodstock and held it out to me. "Would you mind?"

"Not at all. See you in a bit, Lucy and Sally." I grabbed the tape off the register as I passed and hung up the poster in the window. The top read, "Celebrate the Great Pumpkin with a latte." I had just attached the last piece of tape when Bear and Henri came in.

"Two lattes please," Henri said as she turned back to me. "Thought you might appreciate some more float-riders."

"Really? Yes, please. The more the merrier."

"Good," Bear said as he held up a child's piano. "I really hope you don't have a Schroeder yet." The big man looked so excited.

"We do not, and we definitely need one. You can ride at the front and play us along." I laughed as Bear grimaced. "I don't mean that you really have to play. We have a recording."

"Whew," Bear said as he plunked down his piano and headed toward the café. "You had me worried."

"Who are you going to be?" I asked Henri.

"Well, do you have a Marcie yet?" she asked.

Behind her Rocky let out a cackle. "I love it. The artist with dreadlocks plays the bookish girl with thick glasses."

Henri laughed. "At least I'm not doing white face, right?"

She put on a huge set of glasses, like the ones clowns wear and tucked her dreads up under themselves. With her orange tunic, she did a very fine Marcie. "You're hired."

"Does that mean my latte is free?" Henri said as she took her cup from her husband.

"Definitely." I smiled at Rocky. "Keep a tally of drinks for the parade assistants. I'll settle up with you later."

Rocky held up a pad of paper. "You got it." I knew Rocky was saving for grad school now that she'd finished her undergrad degree at Salisbury U, and I didn't want her worrying that she'd have to foot the bill for lots of free drinks. Our revenue-sharing plan served us both, but not if I gave everything away.

Henri, Bear, and I headed out to Main Street with our lattes and took a seat on the bench in front of the store. All along the side-walk, other stores were putting out tables with sale items or giveaways. Next door, the man who owned the garden center was setting out a bazillion tiny pots filled with succulents. I walked over to take a look and ended up buying five on the spot. At a dollar a piece, they were a steal, and I knew just the place in our side yard that I wanted them.

A couple of doors down, the men who ran the hardware store had set up a mini-workshop where kids could build their own toolboxes. And down the other way, at Elle's place, I saw she had buckets of flower stems on a table. At Chez Cuisine, I saw Symeon out front with a portable griddle, and I couldn't resist seeing what he was making.

As I sauntered over, I kept an eye out for Max since I was not yet caffeinated enough to tactfully fend him off, but the smell of whatever Symeon was making distracted me. Just as I reached the griddle, I was assaulted from behind by breath on the back of my neck and a voice saying, "Bonjour, Belle" at my ear.

I cringed and spun with my hand out to keep Max from getting closer. "Good Morning, Max." I turned quickly to Symeon. "What are you making?"

"Omelettes, of course." He pointed to the light circle of egg in front of him. "Want one?"

My stomach growled my response. "Yes, please." I looked at the containers of fillings he had on ice beside him. "Mushrooms and cheddar, please."

Max groaned beside me. "You would prefer swiss, would you not? Symeon, please."

Symeon looked at me and winked. "The lady knows what the lady wants," he said as he sprinkled cheddar on my omelette and dropped a few mushrooms onto the griddle before adding them to the eggs and cheese and folding everything over.

"Yes, she does." A voice said beside me as a hand slipped around my waist. Daniel.

"I do, indeed." I leaned over and kissed my boyfriend on the cheek then looked pointedly at Max.

He harrumphed and walked away, and I could feel Daniel smiling beside me.

"Make one for you?" Symeon asked Daniel.

"Oh yes. Ham and cheddar, please."

In a few moments, Symeon had made two perfect omelettes and served them onto paper plates with compostable silverware. He pointed us to a small table beside his cook station, and Daniel and I sat down to savor our surprise breakfast. It was still early, so Symeon turned down the gas on the griddle and gestured to a stool beside the table, "Do you mind?"

Daniel smiled. "Please. Least we can do to share someone else's table with the person who made us breakfast."

Symeon perched on the stool. "Thanks." A yawn stretched his face. "Whew, I am not used to daytime hours."

"I expect not. Restaurant hours are brutal," I said as I stifled a yawn myself. "Seems like you love what you do, though?"

"I do. A lot." He looked over my shoulder and frowned. "Mostly, anyway."

I glanced behind me and saw Tuck headed our way. I looked back at Symeon. "You okay?"

A long sigh slid through Symeon's lips. "Yeah. Just spent a lot of time talking with the sheriff last night. Seems like he might be considering me as a suspect in my uncle's murder."

I shot Daniel a quick glance, and he was studying a tiny piece of ham on his place. "Oh, well, that must be disconcerting." I felt like *disconcerting* might not even begin to describe what he was feeling, but it was the best I could do if I was, indeed, chatting with an omelette-making murderer. "Any idea why he thinks that?"

Daniel kicked me under the table in the universal symbol for "Stop being nosy," but I chose to ignore him and glanced back to see that Tuck had stopped to chat with the agents from the real estate office a couple of doors up.

Symeon shrugged. "It's no secret that my uncle and I didn't get along. But I guess the sheriff just discovered that we'd had a fight last weekend." A flush of color crept up from under Symeon's beard. "A big fight."

"Oh," I said and kind of wished I'd paid attention to Daniel's kick. I didn't want to think another of my new friends might be a murderer. Still, I found myself talking before I could stop myself. "Fight about what?"

"About what a total and complete misogynist he is." Symeon cracked his knuckles. "I didn't punch him or anything, but I threatened to if he hurt any more women."

"Did you know any of the women he, um, harassed?" I didn't know if it was wise to let Symeon know about his uncle's more violent behaviors if he was a suspect.

"I did. And it wasn't just harassment, as bad as that was—"

"Well, hello Harvey. Daniel," Tuck's greeting was friendly but crisp. "Symeon. Good to see you this morning."

I looked up at my friend the sheriff and smiled. "Good morning, Tuck. You ready for the parade?"

He tilted his head and pursed his lips, but then, he must have decided to let what he overheard go. "As ready as I'll ever be to sit in the back of a convertible and wave at people."

"What?! It's not always been your greatest desire to be the home-coming queen?" Daniel asked with a smirk.

"Hardly," Tuck said. "The parade is fun, though, and I'm loving all the folks who have set up on the street." He eyed the griddle. "Any chance I can trouble you?"

Symeon stood up with a smile. "Sure. What can I do you for?"

"Is that crepe batter I see?" Tuck pointed at a stainless steel tub that I had totally overlooked.

"As a matter of fact it is," Symeon said as he ladled a circle of the batter onto the griddle. "Sweet or savory?"

I moaned. "I didn't see you had crepes."

Daniel laughed beside me. "Split a sweet one."

I smiled. "Perfect."

A few minutes later, Tuck had his ham and cheddar crepe in a cone-shaped holder, and Daniel and I were passing a Nutella and banana one back and forth between us as we headed back toward the shop. We'd decided we'd all gather behind the shop at eight forty-five so that we could ride around together to the staging area, which was set up in the parking lot behind Daniel's garage.

As we passed through my store, Marcus gave me a wave from the register. He was wearing a Peanuts T-shirt with Franklin on the front. "Nice shirt," I shouted.

"Thanks. My girlfriend bought it for me. Said I could wear the token even if I couldn't be one." He laughed, and I saw Rocky giving me a thumbs up behind him.

My heart cracked with joy when I walked out and saw our float.

Not only did the float itself look amazing with the huge pumpkin Cate had made and the doghouse that Woody and I had crafted, but everyone in costume made me so happy. Daniel had slipped on his bald cap as we walked out, and now with a sharpied curly-cue of hair on his head and his yellow T-shirt with the brown stripe, he looked perfect. Bear was hunched over his toy piano, with Henri as Marcie by his side. Mart and Tiffany were sitting at the front of the float with their gigantic wigs and the exact outfits that Lucy and Sally wore in most of the show's episodes. And Woody was at the very back end of the trailer, and when I looked at him, he tossed a handful of powder in the air, swathing himself in a cloud of dust. Pig-Pen incarnate. Mom and Dad had bowed out on the pretense that the float was becoming overcrowded and their presence would only "dilute the effect." I wasn't upset. In fact, my sometimes-too-serious parents might have disrupted our silliness game big time.

Daniel went over and untied Mayhem and Taco from the telephone pole where we'd left them with water and helped Mayhem into her costume. That dog was so good-natured that she let us slip a giant yellow cowl on her head before we lifted her to her place next to Mart. Taco, however, was not as easygoing. He was not eager to climb up onto his fancy dog bed on the doghouse . . . until we showed him that Tiffany was holding an entire bag of bacon bits. Then, he was very eager.

I pulled the jar of pomade out of the tote full of candy I had brought to throw to the crowd and gave my hair a good slicking to straighten it out a bit. Then, I climbed up onto the float, leaned a hip against Taco's doghouse, and braced myself.

THE PARADE WAS A BLAST. People loved our float, and of course, Taco, Mayhem, and Pig-Pen stole the show. I gave out all my candy in the first ten minutes, but fortunately, Mart had planned ahead and stashed lots of hard candies around us. So we threw candy and waved, and the sign advertising the store at the back flapped in the wind the whole time. I saw a lot of faces I knew in the crowd, but there were far more visitors than residents, so by the time we parked back behind the shop, I was hopeful we'd have a good weekend of sales.

And if the crowd inside was any indication, it was going to be our best weekend yet. It didn't hurt that we had the toddler-sized "First In Parade" Blue Ribbon now on display in the window.

Marcus was ringing up a huge purchase of what looked to be the Warrior Cats series for a young girl and her mother, and other customers were all around the store. He had things well in hand, but Rocky was swamped. I quickly dropped my tote behind the register and went to help her out by ringing sales. I couldn't froth up a Snoopy, but I could count change.

As the parade crowd started to wander in, Mart took over at the register for Marcus so that he could help customers find books, and Daniel helped her bag purchases. Henri had to get back to her art studio at the co-op to give tours, but Bear hung around and helped stack books that got left around the shop. A few minutes later, Pickle came in, and soon he and Bear were escorting customers around the store and making them laugh at the same time.

When the crowd finally wound down a bit, I went to inspect the goodie bag tables out front and heard fits of laughter. I peeked around the corner into the parking lot and saw Woody, dust cloud ablazing, with a crowd around him like he was a magician at a child's birthday party. "Who knew that my piles of lathe dust would be such a hit?" he said.

"Oh, that's what that is. I wondered if you'd been gathering dust from our neighbors to have such a supply."

He laughed and tossed another handful. "By the way, Cate has a surprise for you. She's sending Lucas with it shortly, she said."

I looked at him out of the corner of my eye. "Do you know what the surprise is, sir?"

"I have delivered my message," he looked at the crowd of children gathered around him, "but now if you'll excuse me, my fan club awaits." Another puff of dust went into the air as I turned to head back to the store.

I didn't have to wait long to learn about Cate's surprise. Within a few minutes, Lucas, Stephen, and Walter had appeared in front of the shop with the giant pumpkin behind them on a wagon. From my spot at the register – Mart had needed to head to the winery to prepare for the fundraiser – I could see they parked it on the sidewalk next to the front door, and a minute later, Stephen came in and said, "We need your muscles."

I furrowed my brow, shrugged at Marcus, and headed out. There, Walter stood with a sledgehammer. He grinned at me and put the handle in my hands. "The honor is all yours," he said as he pointed at Cate's beautiful pumpkin.

"What?! No. I'm not destroying that. It's too beautiful." I tried to hand the sledge back to Walter, who refused it by putting his hands behind his back.

"You heard the man. Smash the thing," Cate said as she stepped through the crowd toward me. "I can make you a new one, but you need to smash this one."

I stared at my tiny friend, and she nodded again. So I swung the hammer over my head and let it fall against the top of the pumpkin, where it promptly glanced off and sent me flying against the planter box behind me. I reached back to steady myself and my hand slipped down into the coleus leaves. That's when I felt a blaze of heat run up my fingers.

When I pulled my hand out of the planter, I was bleeding . . . and holding a huge knife.

10

L ucas looked from me to the knife and back to me again. "Drop it," he said as he walked toward me briskly and put his body between the planter and the crowd.

Stephen swooped in with the literal shirt off his back and wrapped up my bleeding fingers, and Walter whisked the hammer out of my hands. We had an audience, and it wouldn't do for business to have the crowd scared by a bloody knife. My friends knew this before I had even fully registered what happened.

"Oh man, looks like Harvey has suffered a pumpkin-related injury, folks. Looks like Walter and I will have to do the honors," Cate said. "On the count of three. One. Two. Three." As she said three, Walter swung the sledgehammer against the side of the pumpkin, and it broke open, spilling candy all over the sidewalk.

"Enjoy, everyone," Cate said as tiny hands – and not so tiny ones – grabbed for the Smarties and SweeTARTS that had filled the entire massive pumpkin. The town would be on a sugar high for a week.

I noticed all of this, of course, but I couldn't do much about it, what with the bleeding and all. So I let Woody and his less intense puff of dirt escort me inside to the shop's backroom, where he quickly grabbed Rocky to tend me and then got our first aid kit from behind the register. Within minutes, the cut across my three middle fingers was cleaned and bandaged and Daniel was on his way to drive me to the ER in Easton to see if I needed stitches.

Meanwhile, Tuck was already on hand and had bagged the knife and was asking Cate, now that the crowd had thinned, along with the candy, what had happened. "I'm not sure, exactly. She just pulled up her hand, and there was a knife in it." Cate stared at me, and I smiled, although I imagine it came out as more of a wince.

"I don't know what happened exactly," I said as Tuck pulled a chair up beside me. "I fell against the planter, and when I went to steady myself, I must have grabbed ahold of the knife."

Tuck wrote something brief in his notepad. "And Elle just filled those boxes yesterday, right? I saw her out there during the fair, I think."

I nodded. "Yep, so someone must have dropped the knife there since then." I tried to wiggle my fingers and felt a lance of pain run up my hand. "But why? Why would someone hide a knife in my planter boxes?"

Tuck blew a rough breath out and stared at me. "Have you been asking questions, Harvey?"

I stared back at him, trying to figure out what he was talking about. "Questions? Questions about what? I don't know what you mean."

A tiny wrinkle formed between the sheriff's eyebrows. "You haven't been sleuthing about Coach Cagle?"

I blushed. "Not really. I mean Symeon was telling me you questioned him last night, but . . . wait! Is that the knife that?" I felt bile rise up in my throat. "Do I have his blood . . . ?" I felt like I was going to pass out, so I put my head down between my legs like they used to tell me to do in gym class when I overdid it with the jump rope and felt faint.

"Deep breaths, Harvey. The hospital will test you and make sure you're okay, but the coach didn't have any communicable diseases." Tuck's voice was professional, which I found soothing.

"You mean he didn't have HIV," Cate said.

"Right. He didn't have HIV. They'll give you antibiotics and test everything at the hospital, Harvey. It's okay." The sheriff was rubbing small circles on my back.

I tried to shake my head to say I wasn't worried – well, I hadn't been worried about HIV. More it was just the idea of someone else's blood in my body, but now I just wanted to get to the hospital and get checked out. The cut was one thing – an illness was entirely another. "Where's Daniel?"

"I'm right here," he said as he rushed in and knelt beside me. "Let's go get you looked at, okay?" He kissed my temple as he helped me to my feet. "Someone call Mart?"

"Already on it," Cate said as she squeezed my forearm. "Lucas is going to stay and help Marcus and Rocky with the store, and Bear and PIckle are taking care of things outside."

"I'm staying too," Woody said, "just in case."

"We've got the shop, Harvey. See you in a little while," Rocky added as the three of us walked to the back door.

I tried to smile with enthusiasm as I left, but I felt so lightheaded and weak that I'm sure I wasn't convincing. I wasn't squeamish about seeing blood or anything, but the idea that I'd – well, I couldn't even think about it.

On the ride to the hospital, Daniel asked me a few questions, mostly about how things were going at the shop with the festival, and I appreciated that he didn't push me on the knife stuff. I didn't feel like talking much though, so despite his quiet nature, he managed to ramble on about his own morning after the parade. He'd set up a small car clinic beside his garage to show locals how to change oil and fill the washer fluid – basic car skills. "Don't worry, though. Ollie took over."

I smiled, then, remembering the kid who lived in the basement of Stephen and Walter's house. We'd helped him out of a bind a few months ago. "Ollie knows how to change the oil in a car?"

"I know, right? Turns out he worked at one of those quick-change car places for a while. He knows a lot." Daniel continued to prattle on about the locals – including Daniel's favorite customer, Mrs. Fenster, who had apparently managed to put seven thousand miles on her car in the last two months despite the fact that she claimed only to drive to the dollar store and back home. Someday we'd solve that mystery. Today, I was content to let Daniel talk so I didn't have to think.

At the hospital, the doctor checked my cut and butterflied it closed. No stitches required. I got two weeks' worth of antibiotics just in case and was told to soak the cut every night in warm soapy water to speed healing. Then, they sent me home. I was in and out in fifteen minutes. Slow day in the ER.

Daniel wanted to take me home. "I'll put on that *Travelers* show you've been wanting me to watch with you, get you a bowl of mint chip ice cream, and spend the afternoon trying to figure out why you like sci-fi tv so much. What do you say?"

That sounded so lovely, but I knew I needed to be at the store. This was, hands-down, the biggest sales day in our almost-one-year history as a bookstore, and I didn't want to miss it. "I need to be at the store, Daniel." Before he could protest, I raised my wounded hand and said, "But I will rest there, okay? I'll just answer questions and fill goodie bags, okay?"

Daniel sighed, but he agreed. And soon I was installed in a wing chair near the front of the store with a small table in front of me. Woody penned me a sign that said, "Ask the Owner," and I spent the afternoon in a delightful series of conversations with customers. In some ways, it was the perfect way for me to spend the afternoon.

By later in the afternoon, I had eaten two of Rocky's mom's cinnamon rolls and had my two other Peanuts'-themed lattes, although on Rocky's suggestion I made the third of the day a decaf. Marcus, with the help of Lucas, Bear, and Pickle, had kept the store humming. We'd even managed to sell some of the legal and medical books that Bear and Pickle had suggested I carry because they had so enthusiastically recommended them. I was especially grateful to move along the copy of *Gray's Anatomy* that Bear had recommended we carry, and I loved that a teenage girl with cinnamon skin and a nose ring had bought it to use for her illustrations and caricatures. Bear looked pleased, too. "At least their kidneys will be in the right place," he said as he told me about the sale.

Mart had called five times to check in, and she kept telling me to skip the gala tonight, that she and Tiffany could manage. I wanted to go, though. It sounded like fun, and I was more than a little invested in the cause given what I was learning about Coach Cagle. Besides, I thought maybe I could get a little more information out of Tiffany, see if I could exonerate her, I hoped. Finally, I convinced Mart that it would be better if I went, that it would keep my mind off my hand, and she arranged to have me manage the silent auction, a task I could do with minimal use of my hand. "Besides, you were a fundraiser for years. Maybe you can get the bid up."

"I can definitely do that. See you at six," I told my best friend and looked at my watch. It was four thirty, which meant I had just enough time to get home, feed Mayhem and myself, and get into my one and only fancy dress, before Tiffany arrived to go to the winery. I was glad I hadn't cut my foot because limping was not an option given what the next ninety minutes demanded.

I checked in with Marcus, who was totally on top of everything, even with three of his trusty assistants gone. "Woody and I have got this, Harvey. You just go enjoy yourself." He patted my uninjured hand.

"And be sure to take a selfie in that dress," Rocky shouted from the café.

I rolled my eyes and whistled for Mayhem. She and Taco trotted out from their sleeping place of choice behind the psychology section, and I hooked up their leashes before carefully placing them in my left hand. I hoped no errant rabbits crossed our path on the way home because my left hand was nowhere near strong enough to keep two dogs from bolting after their prey.

I needn't have worried, though, because I was barely out the door when Daniel caught up to me and took the leashes. "I heard you were going to be hotter than usual tonight," he said as he took hold of my hand. "Mind if I escort you?"

I sighed. "Mart texted you."

"Of course. I am officially on the guest list as the 'Silent Auction Attendant's Valet.'"

"Ooh la la," I said. "I've never been so fancy, but you, sir, are not nearly fancy enough." I looked at his oil-stained coveralls. "Unless you're about to pull a James Bond on me and say you have a tux under those things."

He laughed. "You only wish." He glanced over his left shoulder at the street. "But it's almost as good."

Just then, Ollie biked up and, without stopping, handed Daniel a suit bag. "Have fun," Ollie said as he pedaled away and left me standing there with my mouth open.

"That was incredible," I said with a laugh.

"I aim to please," Daniel said. "Now, let's get home and get gussied up."

WHEN TIFFANY ARRIVED, I was sitting on the couch alternating mouthfuls of cheddar cheese-covered rice and M&Ms. The fact that I hadn't bothered to decant the candy from the giant tub Mart had picked up at the warehouse store spoke to the way the day had finally gotten to me. I was still looking forward to the night, but I was tired, physically and psychologically.

Tiffany looked about the way I felt. Her dress was gorgeous – bright red silk that draped and hugged beautifully on her long, lean runner's body. Earlier in my life, I might have been jealous or self-conscious in the company of a woman who fit the stereo-types of beauty that Americans treasured, but a few decades of self-care, a few relationships with women who were gorgeous physically but atrocious as people, and a few really hard conver-sations that revealed all women struggle with our own sense of beauty and I found myself feeling pretty good about how I looked in my empire-waisted black dress with a tulle underlay. The thin band of silver sequins along my rib cage made me feel dressed up but was still true to my no-frills personal style.

And if I'd had any doubt that I was beautiful, Daniel would have dispelled that immediately when he came in and smiled with the most tender, perfect glow in his eyes. He spoke to Tiffany politely, but his eyes rarely left me – and that felt amazing. Plus, he looked gorgeous in his charcoal gray suit and a burgundy bowtie. We were going to make a fine pair of silent auction attendants.

After putting away my stress-driven "supper," I threw Taco and Mayhem each a bone and made sure their water bowl was full. Then, I fluffed up Aslan's favorite cashmere throw on the sofa and put a saucer with a little tuna on top of the fridge. The dogs wagged their tails gratefully, and Aslan showed her gratitude by curling up with her back to me on her blanket. "See you guys later," I said as we headed out.

Daniel drove my truck with me beside him and Tiffany next to the passenger window. I loved the idea of us in our fancy outfits in this vintage truck, and apparently, we put on a good show because when we pulled up the actual valet, not to be confused with Daniel as my personal valet, whistled as we stepped out. Quite a few other heads turned, and I decided that I was going to put the knife incident out of my mind and enjoy the night.

When we stepped inside, the room was buzzing with people laying out flatware and adjusting tablecloths. In one corner, I saw Elle and waved. She was finagling the centerpieces on the main buffet table, and once again, she had created amazing work – big bouquets of sunflowers in all varieties. And on the dining tables themselves, she had placed tiny vases of dried strawflowers surrounded by the smallest pumpkins and gourds I'd ever seen. It was tasteful and perfect for a setting where it was important that people talk without being blocked from each other by huge flower arrangements.

Mart came bustling over, and despite how much she was responsible for, she looked amazing in a short, electric-blue cocktail dress and strappy sandals, and her hair was swept up with a rhinestone-encrusted clip on one side. The only blemish on her was the frown she wore as she came over and grabbed my right wrist. "Let me see," she said.

I turned my hand so that the cut was facing her, but I'd hidden the bandages under a black scarf I'd twisted with a thin silver ribbon and wrapped around my hand. "Like my new accessory? I call it "hospital chic." I grinned.

"Well, clearly if you can make bad jokes, you are okay. You are okay, right?" Her eyes bore into mine.

"I am totally fine. Now, where do you need us?"

Mart gave me one last look and then snapped her focus back to the event. "Tiffany, are you up for welcoming guests?"

"Whatever you need," Tiffany said. "Just point me in the right direction."

"Great. Actually, you'll all be kind of together right here." She pointed at a long table. "Tiffany, here's your clipboard. All you need to do is say Hello to everyone, and check off their names when they come in."

"Got it," Tiffany replied and took a position near the door with a wink to me. "No one gets past me without a welcome."

I laughed and once again hoped she wasn't a killer. But I couldn't ponder that possibility long because Mart was talking to me, and I was missing my directions.

". . . so that's it. Pretty simple, right?" Her eyes were wide as she looked from me to Daniel.

"Totally simple," Daniel answered for both of us. "We've got it, Mart."

"Awesome. Thank you all. Doors open in," she looked down at her silver watch, "ten minutes. Dinner begins at seven, so if you could get as many bids as possible in that half-hour . . ."

"No problem," I said, praying that Daniel had actually heard the directions for what we were supposed to do. "Do we have a goal for the silent auction?"

Mart grinned. "That's my girl. Does ten thousand seem too high?"

I looked at the table full of gift certificates, hand-thrown pots, and gift baskets. "Depends. Any big ticket items?"

"Does a week's stay at the Biltmore Estate count as big ticket? What about season tickets for the Ravens?" She turned to me with a glimmer in her eye. "Or a week on a luxury yacht with a full crew?"

"Okay, now you're just showing off. You weren't serious about only getting ten thousand for those things were you?"

Mart frowned. "Actually, I was. Silent auctions don't usually bring big money."

"Well, no, not if they are for bottles of wine or St. Michael's tchotchkes. But for those, let's aim for fifty thousand at least."

Mart took a quick step back. "Are you serious?"

"Totally serious. I mean you have some big hitters coming tonight, right? I mean you were talking about some big CEOs last week, billionaires?"

"Shhh. They like to be low-key." Mart blushed. "But yeah . . . One of them donated the yacht, though, so he probably won't bid."

Daniel laughed. "If you can afford to donate a week on your yacht with staff, you can bid on other things. Harvey's right, Mart."

"Alright then," Mart said with a wide spread of her arms. "Let's do this."

As she walked away, I leaned over between Daniel and Tiffany said, "I didn't want to freak her out, but we're going to bring in one hundred K tonight."

Tiffany's eyes got wide. "You're serious?"

"Totally serious. Donors are warm at this kind of event. It won't take much to get them bidding. You welcome them and send them our way," I tilted my head at Daniel. "We'll get their bids."

Daniel looked at me out of the corner of his eye. "What am I going to do? I know nothing about fundraising."

"Ah, but you look like a million bucks. You are our decoy. Just pretend to be considering your bids. I've got the rest.

BY THE TIME Mart welcomed everyone and invited them to the tables for dinner, Daniel and I were well past fifty thousand in bids. It didn't take much to convince people who had already paid five hundred a plate to give more for a great cause. And even those folks who couldn't afford the big items were happy to put down a bit of cash for those bottles of wine and tickets to the local theater. Bidding would close just before dessert was served, and with one more push from me – with Mart's permission – as the entrees came out, I knew we'd be there.

I popped over to where Mart was describing the winery's selections and awards to guests who were interested in joining their wine club and whispered in her ear. She furrowed her brow and then nodded before holding up one finger.

A few moments later, she headed toward the stage and tilted her head for me to follow. She asked the pianist who had been playing throughout the evening to pause for a moment, and then she handed me a microphone.

I smiled as I tried to not trip over my own feet climbing the stairs to the stage, and then I took the microphone. I didn't have a planned speech, but I'd long ago learned that heartfelt, personal messages were the key to great fundraising. So I started with what I felt most at this moment.

"When I moved to St. Marin's just over a year ago, I knew I loved the look and feel of the town. It's quaint and warm, and the landscape is gorgeous. What I didn't know was that I was going to move into the most amazing, supportive community of people I've ever known. When you all see a need, you address it, as is evidenced here tonight by your presence."

I looked across the crowd and saw the gentle smiles of people who had been complimented sincerely.

"Just by coming tonight, you have done a great work and given RAINN funds they need to continue their support of people who are the victims of sexual violence. Thank you." I watched lots of heads nod at tables around the room and assumed those were the RAINN staff.

"Now, I'm asking you – if you are able – to give a little more. We have some amazing prizes over at the Silent Auction." I pointed toward the long table, and Daniel did his best Vanna White impression, hand wave and all, to show off the high-ticket items. "We need to honor the gifts of our donors by getting the bidding going on these items. Let me tell you about a few of them."

I then did my best sales pitch for how good someone would feel at every Raven's game this season if they knew those seats bought people safety from abusive situations, and how wonderful it would be to invite friends on a week-long yacht cruise if you could tell them their vacation was supporting people who really needed that support. I could see people looking from me to the table as I talked, and finally, I sensed the right moment – the moment when the pitch would land. I'd never be a car salesman, but I could sell the crap out of a good cause.

"So who's going to take these moments before dessert to change the lives of men and women who really need a win in the world? I don't need a show of hands. Nope, I need you to move your feet." I smiled and made eye contact with someone at each table, and within a few seconds, I heard the sound of a chair moving back, then another, and then more. Soon, at least a dozen people were over at the silent auction, filling out their bids.

I cleared my throat loudly to pull the attention back to me for one last minute, the last clincher to guarantee we'd hit our goal. "Bidding will close when the dancing opens, so don't wait. If you want that good feeling that comes from doing something really amazing, now is the time." A few last-minute folks jumped up, and I said, "Thank you."

Before I left the stage, I quickly made arrangements with the band leader to give a five minute "bids are closing" warning and then announce the end of the auction.

When I handed the mic back to Mart, she looked panicky. "You're closing the bidding."

I pursed my lips. "I thought that was your plan all along."

She winced. "Well, it was the plan, but I didn't really intend to stick to it. I thought we'd just let people keep bidding to make more."

I shook my head. "Nope, it doesn't work that way. People will intend to bid but then forget after they've had a little more wine or when they realize they need to get home to the sitter. You've got to close the deal early in the evening." I gave her a hug. "Plus, then you get to announce what the auction's proceeds are. People get even more generous when they know they're in a crowd of generous people."

Mart had twisted a single strand of hair around her index finger, and it looked like it was cutting off the circulation. "Trust me,

Mart. I'm good at this, remember?" I put my hands on her shoulders. "I'll bring you the total in a half hour. Worst case scenario, you can ask for final donations to close the gap as you give the final thanks at the end of the night." I winked and headed back toward Daniel.

My boyfriend was schmoozing so well that I almost didn't want to interrupt. He was pointing people toward the high-price items while also mentioning that the money spent the same even if it was applied to a really good bottle of wine. I gave his bicep a squeeze as I passed by, and he smiled. This was definitely not his thing, but he always rose to the occasion.

I took my place at the end of the table and encouraged people to bid generously – but always within their means. I looked up websites on my phone to give the bidders thorough information about the items up for auction, and I even helped one woman whose arthritis had stolen her ability to write make a ridiculously generous bid on a tea gift basket. "I do love tea," she said with a wink and a smile.

When the five-minute warning came, every item had a sizable bid, and there was an all-out bidding war over the week's yacht rental. The amounts these two men were putting down left me breathless because they were more than my bookstore would *gross* in a year, but I was also breathless with excitement. From just my quick tally, I could tell we'd surpassed our goal. I couldn't wait to see what our total was.

At the very last second, a middle-aged woman in sensible pumps and a suit dashed over to grab the pen on the yacht rental. She stood poised, and as the band leader closed the auction, she put down her final bid. I tried not to stare, but her fanfare made that impossible. And so did her bid – one million! I started to cry. Mart was going to be ecstatic.

The woman started to dart away as soon as her bid was done,

but both Daniel and I went after her. He was faster, so he stepped in front of her as she headed toward the front doors. "Ma'am, I just wanted to say thank you," he said. I stepped beside him and smiled.

She stopped, looked him in eye, and said, "No need. A person on the phone at RAINN saved my life fifteen years ago. I'm just passing along the gift." Then, she walked past us and left. I had to take deep breaths to keep from sobbing. I didn't want to embarrass myself, but more, I didn't want Mart to worry. From me, tears could mean anything from sheer terror to anger to sadness to complete joy. She didn't need to be focused on me, so I took one more deep breath and gathered the bidding sheets.

As the dance floor began to fill, Daniel and I started to tally. I cannot even add two two-digit numbers without a calculator, so I was very glad for my phone for the second time that night. We wrote down each winning bid and who had placed it, and then we ran a total for proceeds. We ran it a second and a third time just to be sure. When we were sure, we stared at one another wide-eyed for a few seconds, and then we tried to walk casually to where Mart was sitting.

I don't know what she saw in our faces, but she jumped up when we came over and reached for the paper in Daniel's hand. "I think you need to sit down, Mart," Daniel said.

Her face fell. "That bad, huh?"

"Well, not exactly. I pulled her down into her seat and sat down, turning a chair to face her." I laid the tally sheet in front of her and waited.

She looked at the figure and tilted her head. Then, she picked it up and brought it closer to her face before running her finger down the list of dollar figures and setting the sheet down again. "That can't be right. You must have miscalculated."

"Nope," I said. "We triple-checked, and we personally witness that last number get written down. The Silent Auction brought in $1,585,000, Mart."

My friend is not a crier, but tears welled in her eyes. "How? What?! How is that possible?"

Daniel sat down on the other side of her and told her about the bidding wars and the people who bid up prices just to get others to bid higher, too. Then, he told her about the woman who wanted to thank RAINN. "It's amazing, huh?" he said as he squeezed Mart's hand.

"I can't believe it. I have to go tell the director." She turned to me and let out a shuddering breath. "What do I say?"

I smiled. "You tell her that her budget is covered for the next few years."

Mart slammed me to her chest. "Thank you, Harvey."

"Oh, no, don't thank me. Thank RAINN. Their work is what made people give. Just tell them to keep it up." I felt myself choking up again, so I stopped talking.

"Alright. This is going to be so fun." Mart wiped a tear off her cheek and headed toward a tall woman who was dancing with her wife in the middle of the dance floor.

Daniel scooted over next to me, and we watched with no shame at all as that tall woman broke down on her wife's shoulder as Mart whispered in her ear. "That's what joy looks like," Daniel said.

"Yes. Yes it is," I said. "Care to dance?" "More than Words" by Extreme was playing, and I couldn't help but sing along, harmony even. My choir teacher had used this nineties hit all the time, and I still loved it. Plus, it was fun to sing it to Daniel as we turned in small circles around the crowded dance floor.

Eventually, the dance floor began to clear, and Mart took to the stage to thank everyone for coming. "We are so grateful to all of you, and we are thrilled to announced that we raised over \$2.1 million for RAINN tonight, thanks to your generosity in both buying tickets and especially for those wonderful silent auction bids. Now, someone else wants to say thank you." The director took the microphone from Mart and told the gathered benefactors that these funds would cover operating expenses for the next two years AND allow the organization to expand its hotline staff and their educational program to college campuses. Tears flowed down her face as she spoke, and I saw a number of people wiping their eyes as well. The night had been a success on all accounts.

Tiffany had been an amazing greeter, and many people shook her hand as she left, thanking her for her hospitality. She was gracious and resisted the temptation that I would have had to explain that really I was just a volunteer. When the last guests left, she offered to stay and help Mart wrap up and suggested I get on home. "You have had a huge weekend, and you still have to open the shop tomorrow," she said.

I yawned and nodded. I wanted to stay and help – helping made me happy – but I knew that I needed to respect my own needs and head home, so I hugged Mart and took Daniel's arm as we headed toward the car.

A blood-curdling scream rang out across the parking lot just as Daniel opened my door, and I knew that my night of rest wasn't in the cards.

11

It didn't take long for us to figure out who was screaming and why. There, scrawled in bright blue paint along the foundation at the front of the club were the words, "Those girls were asking for it." I hissed when I saw the graffiti, something inside me clenching at the ways those words had been thrown at me and other people I knew who had been assaulted.

The person screaming was Tiffany, and she hadn't stopped. I rushed over to her, put my arm around her waist and turned her away. Tears were pouring down her face, and I wasn't sure she had taken a breath in the minute or so it had taken me to reach her. Daniel took us both by a shoulder and steered us back into the parking lot, where he opened the truck door and helped me get Tiffany inside. I squeezed in next to her, and Daniel got behind the wheel.

With Tiffany squeezed between us, Daniel pulled around to the side of the building and then quickly dialed Tuck while I encouraged our friend to take deep breaths. Within a few moments, she was breathing more normally and had stopped crying. But then, her jaw clenched in what I recognized as rage, and I couldn't blame her. Someone had the audacity to come to an event for an organization that helped the victims of sexual assault and scrawl a victim-blaming message – that someone had a lot of nerve . . . and a lot of rage.

I could feel the threads of some understanding beginning to knit together at the back of my mind, but I didn't have space or energy to attend to them yet. Right now, Tiffany needed me, and Tuck was going to need our statements.

Daniel tilted his head toward the building, and I nodded. One of us needed to let Mart know what was going on – if she wasn't already aware. Plus, if I read his look correctly, he wanted me to figure out why Tiffany had come outside after she had said she was staying behind to help. Something wasn't adding up here, and it was time to divide and conquer.

"Daniel is going to get Mart, Tiffany, okay?" I rubbed tiny circles in a counterclockwise motion on her back in the way my mom said her Reiki practitioner suggested was calming. "I'm so sorry you saw that. Are you okay?"

Tiffany took a big, shuddering breath and nodded slowly. "I am. Or I will be. I think." His voice was tiny. "I just came out to catch you so I could grab my bag from the truck . . ." Her voice trailed off.

I pushed myself up in the seat and saw Tiffany's duffel with her clothes from earlier. "You wanted to change for clean-up," I said. That made perfect sense, and the gnawing pit of suspicion in my belly faded away. "Well, what do you say we head in and get you into your jeans? I'll find a coffee pot, too."

Tiffany briefly rested her head on my shoulder. "Thanks, Harvey." Then she frowned and looked me in the eye. "No, wait. You need to get home and rest. That was the whole point of you leaving."

I stepped out of the truck and grabbed Tiffany's bag. "I'm

already on it," I said as I pulled my phone from the glovebox of the truck. "Marcus will be fine to open." I hoped I was right as I texted him. His response was immediate. "Rocky and I R on it. Keep me posted?"

I replied and then tucked my phone into my bra and felt like one of those tough old women who keep their cash up there. Then, I tucked my arm around Tiffany's elbow and led her through the door that Daniel had gone through. When we got inside, we were at the side of the stage, and I could see Mart and Daniel near the front door, talking with one of Tuck's deputies.

I spotted an empty chair by the now-dismantled sound system and pointed to it. I smiled at Tiffany then said, "Go directly to the bathroom to change. Do not pass the front doors. Do not talk to anyone. Return to this seat immediately to collect your, um, two-hundred dollar coffee."

A small smile lifted the corners of Tiffany's mouth, "Clearly, you have played too many rounds of Monopoly?" She lifted her bag and headed toward the bathroom at the back of the room. I watched the swinging door close behind her before I headed toward my friends.

"Tuck's on his way," Daniel said as I walked up. "I already gave our statement."

I nodded and then looked at Mart. "You okay?" The blood had drained from her face, but I expected that was some combination of fatigue and shock.

"I think so. But who would do this, Harvey? I mean it takes a special kind of hate to graffiti a fundraiser," she said.

"It does, and that scares me. I want you all to clear out, okay? We can take care of clean-up tomorrow." Tuck was striding through the front doors, and several deputies came in just after him. "Seriously, we need to empty the building."

I felt my pulse quicken again. Tuck's voice had that "no-nonsense tone" he used when he didn't want to be questioned, so I didn't unfurl the million queries at the back of my tongue. Instead, I glanced around at the couple dozen people in the room and headed toward a cluster of waitstaff who were pulling the linens off the tables and putting them in a rolling bin.

Behind me, I saw Daniel and Mart disperse, too, and within a few minutes, the three of us and Tuck and his team had spread the word that the building needed to be emptied. While Mart gathered her things, Daniel and I waited by the front door. I was hoping Tuck might explain what had just happened before he shoo-ed us out, but I didn't think it likely. He still had the gait of a man with a purpose as he checked the kitchen and coatroom. He clearly had something on his mind.

The sheriff was just poking his head into the men's restroom when I realized Tiffany hadn't come out of the bathroom. I sprinted across the dance floor and reached Tuck just as he knocked on the women's room door. "Tiffany was in there, but she didn't—"

Tuck didn't even wait for me to finish before shouldering open the door and charging in. I was right behind him, but his broad shoulders kept me from seeing anything but Tiffany's feet, one still in a silvery heel, sprawled across the bathroom floor.

"Call 911," Tuck said, and I whipped my phone out from my bra and dialed.

Then, I burst back out the door and screamed for Daniel and Mart. "Tiffany's hurt. Don't let anyone else drive off." Then I went back to my friend.

Fortunately, by the time I came back in, Tiffany was sitting up against a stall door while Tuck squatted beside her. "So no idea then?"

Tiffany shook her head. "I didn't see a thing. I was bending down to slip off my shoe and them somebody clobbered me on the back of the head." She reached a hand back to the base of her skull and winced. "Whatever they hit me with was heavy."

"Why do you say that?" Tuck asked, and I rolled my eyes. Clearly the woman would know if something heavy hit her.

"Because they swung it up at me, I think. It felt like it was swung from below, like someone slung a heavy purse or something." She winced again. "I don't know. Maybe that doesn't make sense, but I don't think they could lift whatever it was over their head."

I sighed. Once again, it was clear I was not a seasoned investigator because I never would have thought to ask that question. I looked around the room . . . nothing seemed out of place, and I didn't see anything heavy.

"You see anything, Harvey?" Tuck was now standing and watching me with a tiny smile on his face.

I gave him a sheepish smile. "I don't—," I started to say then a silver trashcan behind him caught my eye. I had been in the bathroom earlier that evening, and I thought the trashcan had been right beside the door, not by the window beyond the stalls. "I think that's in the wrong place." I pointed.

Tuck slipped gloves on his hands and leaned over the trashcan to look. "Ladies, move quickly toward the door and on out. Take everyone with you."

When Tiffany and I just stared at him, he shouted, "Now."

I grabbed Tiffany by the arms and hauled her to her feet, and then we ran. As soon as we were through the bathroom door, I started shouting, "Get out! Get out! Everyone get out!" I wasn't sure what Tuck had seen in that trashcan, but if it was what I thought it was, we needed to get as far away as fast as we could.

Daniel took one look at us running, Tiffany still in one heel, and took up my shout, amplifying my voice throughout the room. "Get out of the building right now. Everyone!!"

Fortunately, it looked like only the police officers, Daniel, Mart, Tiffany, and I were still inside, so within seconds, we were all out the front door, and a heartbeat later, Tuck burst out, too. "Move back. Get off the steps. Now."

We kept running until we were at the back of the parking lot. For a moment, we all looked at each other, and then all our gazes turned to Tuck. He had just opened his mouth to speak when an enormous explosion rocked the air as the windows of the winery blew out.

Tiffany screamed again, and instinctively I grabbed her and pulled her face into my shoulder. She continued to scream even as the sound of her voice was overcome by the screams of sirens. An ambulance pulled up next to us, and two EMTs jumped out.

"Do you have something to calm her?" Tuck asked the female EMT. The young woman nodded and then took a firm grip on Tiffany's arms before spinning her from my body to her own and leading her to have a seat on the tailgate of the ambulance. She handed Tiffany a bottle of water and some pills, and Mart went to sit with them.

Only then did I think to check on our local sheriff. "Are *you* okay?" I asked as I took hold of his upper arms. "You cut it close in there."

He let out of a long, slow breath. "I took a bomb diffusing workshop once, so I hoped I'd be able to do it. It was a silly risk, but the winery—"

"No building or business is worth your life," Daniel said. "Glad you're okay."

Tuck nodded, and for a minute, I thought I might have seen a shudder in his breath. But then he straightened his shoulders and turned to the deputies beside us. "Time to work the scene, folks," he said, the authority back in his voice.

I glanced over at Tiffany and Mart and then over at Daniel. "Someone was trying to kill Tiffany."

He sighed. "It appears that way. She's very lucky."

"We all are," I said and dropped to the curb with my head on my knees.

THE EVENTS of the next few hours went by in a blur. At some point, Mart called the winery owners to explain what happened, and they were perfect – gracious, kind, and confident that their insurance would cover everything. Their only concerns were that everyone was okay and that RAINN would still get the proceeds from the event.

Fortunately, the director and her wife as well as all the donors had already left that evening, and all the arrangements for donations had already been made, so RAINN wouldn't suffer at all. In fact, I expected that one unintended benefit of the explosion was that RAINN would get more press than ever, and I hoped maybe that would make some good come out of such a horrific night.

Sometime in the night, my parents showed up with yoga pants, a giant T-shirt, and coffee. "It's decaf," Mom said as she pressed a warm travel mug into my hands, "just in case you might actually get a chance to sleep."

I smiled and took a sip. Mom had mixed in a little cocoa and a little cinnamon with the cream and sugar. It was a perfect drink for a cool night. And she'd brought enough for everyone. Once she'd checked on me, confirmed that Daniel, Mart, and I were sound of body and mind, she gave Dad his marching orders, and they moved out into the crowd with a tray full of coffee mugs.

Soon thereafter, Mart jogged over to me – how she had the energy to jog after all this I could not imagine – and said she was going to ride with Tiffany to the hospital. "She needs someone."

"Of course," I said. "Keep us posted?"

Mart nodded crisply and ran back to the ambulance. She waved from her seat next to Tiffany's stretcher as the EMTs closed the door.

I felt a little knot of emotion against the back of my throat as they rode away. *Both of them could have been killed,* I thought. Tears pooled in my eyes, but now was not the time for me to sink into all the emotions that were swirling inside me. There'd be time for that later. Now, we needed to figure out who had tried to kill Tiffany, and I had a strong suspicion that this attempted murder was linked to the actual murder of Coach Cagle. I couldn't tie the two crimes together, though, not yet.

Tuck and his team were still interviewing everyone who had been inside, and the bomb squad from Annapolis was clearing the building as we spoke. I reached down into my bra again, and when Daniel looked at me with one eyebrow askew, I shrugged and said, "No pockets."

He laughed and then led me to the truck, where he draped a towel that we kept inside to wipe the dogs' feet across the windshield. Then, he stationed himself by the passenger side window, which was facing the now bustling police command center, and let me climb in through the driver's side with the tote of clothes Mom had brought. I was eager to get changed, but it had been a number of decades since I'd dressed in a car, and I had clearly lost all the skills I'd acquired during my busy high school years when my social calendar sometimes required me to change from band uniform to baggy jeans in my Toyota Tercel hatchback.

Fortunately, I managed not to lean on the horn until I was decent because everyone assembled looked over when I did. But in a night of wild emotion, the embarrassment I felt then was only a mild twinge.

When I tapped on the glass behind Daniel, he climbed in beside me and handed me my phone. "I trust you have pockets now."

I grinned. "I do." Mom had brought my favorite comfy pants – drawstring, Lycra, and pockets included. "Now, we need some help."

Daniel looked from me to the ever-growing assemblage of police officers and looky-loos from town and back to me again. "We do?"

I waved my phone at the window. "No, sorry. Not with this. We need help figuring out who did this to Tiffany."

"Harvey Beckett." Daniel's voice was low, almost like a growl. "The sheriff has this well in hand."

I nodded. "I know he does. I know." I leaned the side of my face against the dashboard as I watched the police officers dart from tents and vehicles to the building and back. "But I *need* to do something, Daniel. I can't just sit here and act like nothing happened."

"You're not acting like nothing happened, Harvey. You're letting the police do their jobs." He took my hand and pulled me to him. "That could have been you in there." His voice was thick with emotion.

I looked up at him, and for the first time since I'd known him, he had tears in his eyes. "Please, Harvey."

I sighed and gave him a quick kiss before letting my head sink to his chest. "Okay," I said. "You're right."

Daniel grabbed me by the shoulders and pushed me away from him so he could look me in the face.

"What?!" I squeaked.

"Just wanted to be sure you hadn't dozed off and said that in some sort of dream state." He smiled and pulled me against him again.

"Very funny," I murmured.

My phone kept buzzing against my hand while Daniel and I sat and waited for Tuck to give us the word that we could go home. Each time I lifted the screen, I felt Daniel tense, but I made a point of answering each check-in message with the screen facing toward Daniel. One by one, Cate, Henri, Woody, Pickle, and Marcus checked in, and I let them each know that everyone was okay and that I'd see them sometime tomorrow at the store.

As I was sending my last note, this one to Rocky, Tuck strode over to the truck. "Ya'll can go. I got your statements, and it doesn't look like we are going to get a lot more information from anyone there."

I sat up straight. "Don't you need to ask us all about who we might have seen going in and out? Try to figure out who was out of place?"

"Someday, woman, I'm going to send you to the police academy so you can learn how to do real policing, not this TV stuff. " Tuck squeezed my shoulder. "But since you asked, we did check to see if any of the staff saw anyone out of place, and no one did."

"You didn't ask us?" I said with a huff.

"Man, somebody needs sleep," Tuck said with a smile. "I presumed that you, Ms. Detective, would have already told me if you had seen such a person. Was that not a reasonable assumption?"

The last of the fight went out of me. "Sorry. You're right. I didn't see anyone either."

Tuck turned back toward the building. "That's because the person came in through the bathroom window. We found marks where they'd pried open the frame from the outside. They never went anywhere but the women's restroom."

"Ah," Daniel said as he began to shift away from me. "Well, that explains it."

I looked at him and frowned. "No, it doesn't. How did the person know Tiffany would be in there, assuming Tiffany was the target?" I looked at Tuck for confirmation, and he nodded. "So how did they know Tiffany would go in the bathroom?"

Daniel tilted his head as he climbed into the driver's seat of the truck. "Most of us used the bathroom at some point, right?"

"True," Tuck said, "but Harvey's right. He couldn't have hidden in there all night. Someone would have noticed."

"Someone definitely would have noticed a man in the women's bathroom," I said with a smirk.

"Caught that, did you?" Tuck said and sighed. "Yes, we expect the bomber was a man."

"Because they used the heavy trashcan to hit Tiffany?' I asked.

"Because they used the trashcan." Tuck slipped his baseball cap off his head and ran his hand over his shorn hair. "But not a word, Harvey. You, too, Daniel. To keep Tiffany safe, we need to be sure the bomber doesn't get word of anything about our investigation, okay?"

I nodded. "I just promised Daniel I wouldn't do any sleuthing, so don't worry." I stretched my back away from the truck seat. "I'll be good. Now, is it okay if we go home? I'm beat."

"Yes, please go home and rest. I'll come by the shop tomorrow to check on you." He pushed the door of the truck closed and thumped it twice in the universal symbol for "drive safely."

We pulled up to a small canopy that my mom used at festivals when she was volunteering for one of her many causes and found her and Dad elbow deep in sandwich fixings. "Everyone is beginning to get hungry, so we're going to stay a while," she said. "As long as you don't need us," she said.

I would not have dared pull my mother away from her element. She was practically glowing at the thought of being able to help people. "Nope, I'm all set. Just going to go home and get some sleep. See you all at the shop tomorrow afternoon?"

Dad walked over and put his hand through the truck window. "Glad you're okay, Harvey. We'll bring lunch for everyone tomorrow." He waved a half-made ham and cheese sandwich at the table full of veggies, meats, cheese, and breads. Then he leaned in and gave me a one-armed hug. He smelled like his aftershave and mustard. He smelled like comfort.

ON THE RIDE back into town, my mind kept spinning, trying to figure out how someone had managed to spray paint the front of the winery and also pry open the bathroom window without being seen. People were in and out of both the front doors and the bathroom all night. There wasn't a big window of time for someone to do either crime. And while it now seemed less likely that Tiffany had been specifically targeted – how could they have known she'd be in the bathroom just then? – I couldn't shake the suspicion that this had been about her, that someone was after her specifically.

I was so tired that my mind just kept spinning the same questions and the same images – blue paint on the wooden winery wall, the trashcan, the knife from the planter box at my shop, Tiffany's screaming face.

I could feel my heart rate beginning to climb and knew I had to break through this thought spiral if I had any hope of getting some sleep tonight. So I did what I always did when I needed to calm down. I counted backwards from one thousand. It was a trick my dad had taught me when I couldn't sleep as a kid. "You might get to one too fast if you start at one hundred, but if you start at one thousand, you'll be asleep long before you've counted all the way down," he said, and he was right.

I leaned my head back against the seat and pictured a giant, puffy paint 1,000, then a 999, 998, 997 . . . by the time Daniel pulled in my driveway, my heartrate was normal, and my mind had begun to do that thing it does before sleep, where it starts telling me stories that will become dreams. If I could just get to my bed without incident, I'd be asleep instantly.

"Stay on the couch tonight," I said to Daniel as he helped me out of the truck. I wasn't asking, and he knew it.

He nodded and followed me through the front door. It was so late that our dogs barely thumped their tails from their dog beds by the front window. I grabbed the extra pillow from my bed and flipped open the trunk full of comfy blankets that we used as a coffee table and handed them to Daniel. "Make yourself at home," I said as sleep threatened to steal me right there.

Daniel gave me a kiss on the cheek and then headed to the couch, giving Aslan a gentle shove off her end before folding her throw and dropping it onto the floor. The cat huffed and then padded down the hall behind me as if to say, "You know I sleep with her anyway. You can have that stupid couch" to Daniel.

I slipped off the yoga pants, pulled a headband over my unruly hair, and dropped into bed. I was barely awake a few seconds later when Aslan curled against the back of my legs.

12

The next morning, I woke to the smell of bacon and coffee and smiled. The bacon smelled almost done – I was proud of myself for knowing how "almost done" bacon smelled – so I just slipped my yoga pants back on and headed to the kitchen. I had expected to see Mart at the stove, but she was sitting on a barstool watching Daniel scramble eggs. I felt a flush climb my neck. That guy looked good with a spatula.

Mart grabbed the coffee pot from the counter near her and poured me a cup, adding a liberal helping of cream and sugar just like I preferred. Then, she slid the mug along the counter like we were in a classic movie bar scene, and I scooped it up with aplomb. The world was feeling right this morning.

But then, I saw the circles under Mart's eyes and realized that Daniel was still wearing his suit pants and his undershirt, and I felt the mat of my unwashed and uncombed hair shift on my head. The previous night came flooding back, and I dropped onto the stool next to Mart with a groan. "Did you sleep at the hospital?"

Mart nodded and took a long sip of her coffee. "Fortunately, there was an extra bed in Tiffany's room, so I caught a few good hours. Well, a few hours between all the times they came in and woke Tiffany up to see if she was resting comfortably." Mart rolled her eyes.

I remembered when my dad had knee surgery. All night after the procedure, the nurses had to come in every two hours to check his blood pressure and temperature. Both of us were glad he only had to stay overnight because the sleep in the hospital was not ideal, not at all.

Daniel gave each of us two slices of perfectly crisp bacon and a spoonful of eggs before making himself a plate.

I took one bite of the eggs and moaned. "Did you put cream cheese in these?" I shoveled in another forkful. "They are amazing."

"My aunt Judy always made her eggs that way." He shoved his last piece of bacon into his mouth whole and walked back to the griddle and laid out the rest of the pound.

I must have looked puzzled because Mart said, "Everyone's on their way over for breakfast."

"Oh," I said with a grimace at Daniel. I wasn't sure he was going to be thrilled with talking about this with folks, especially after our discussion last night. "Is that okay with you?"

"Okay with it?" Mart said. "It was his idea."

I felt something pull in my neck when I whipped my head back around to look at Daniel. "You did?!"

He shrugged. "I figured everyone was going to be talking about it anyway, so we might as well talk about it together." He flipped the bacon over with our tongs and said, "I invited Tuck, too. I didn't want any secret sleuthing or anything." He winked at me.

"Got it." I swallowed the rest of my coffee and stood up. "How long do I have?"

Mart looked at the microwave clock. "Ten minutes."

"Just enough time to tame the beast," I said with a pat on my hair.

Nine minutes later, I reemerged with my hair contained in a bandana, my face freshly washed, and a spray of my favorite scent to mask the fact that I had not had time to shower. As I went to check the front window to see who was going to get there first, the doorbell rang, and the door opened immediately after. My mother and father came in with platters of food. "Told you we'd bring lunch," Mom said as she kissed the air near my face and moved on through to the kitchen. Dad gave me an actual hug and then picked up the jugs of lemonade and iced tea to follow after Mom. I smiled. My dad had been a CEO at his own company, but it was clear who was in charge in their house. And it was also clear that he didn't mind that at all.

Soon after, Cate and Lucas, Henri and Bear, Woody, Pickle, Stephen and Walter, and Elle arrived. Everyone grabbed a plate and beginning filling it with the fixings of a world-class brunch. Somehow, we ended up with five-bean salad, green salad, and the Southern concoction of marshmallows and fruit that is sometimes called a salad but is really known more aptly as ambrosia.

I had just eaten, but of course that didn't stop me from filling another plate with the more lunch side of the brunch . . . well, that and more bacon. Soon, we were all perched around the living room with our plates, and it was only then that I realized Tuck wasn't here yet. "Daniel, do you know when the—?"

The doorbell rang at that exact moment, and Mart jumped up to let in Tuck and Lu. "We brought dessert," Lu said with a lilt to her voice. "Do you mind?" She nodded toward the kitchen and looked at Mart and me.

"Please. Make yourself at home," I stood to help her find spoons for the adorable ramekins she'd brought. "Is this your flan?"

Lu winked. "Of course. We all need custard just now."

"I couldn't agree more," I said as I carried the tray of bowls into the kitchen and bent to let each of our friends take a dish. Lu followed with spoons and soon everyone was moaning with delight . . . or overfullness. It was hard to tell.

But the satiated bliss of good food didn't last long. "How is Tiffany?" Mom asked, looking from me to Mart.

"She's okay. Terrified, but coping as well as anyone could expect," Mart said. She turned to Tuck. "Thanks for sending someone to guard her room. I don't think she would have slept a wink without that."

"No problem. I'm glad it helped, but it's also necessary," Tuck said.

"So you are certain she was the target?" I asked, eager to clarify my own thoughts from the previous night.

Tuck nodded. "We are. I can't say why just yet, but we have evidence that confirms she was the target."

I bit my tongue to keep from asking what evidence. I had heard Tuck say he couldn't share that information, and I needed to respect that. For now.

"But why? I mean she's pretty new here. Why go after her?" Cate asked.

"We're still figuring that part out. I don't know her well enough to determine why someone would have come after her specifically, but some of you know her better. Any guesses?" Tuck looked around the room, but eventually his gazed rested on me.

"I don't know what of what I know might be useful, but I can tell you what I've learned." I glanced at Mart. "Given the circumstances, it's probably okay, right?"

Mart nodded. "I actually asked Tiffany this morning if we could share."

Mart looked at Mom who looked at me. I then told everyone about Coach Cagle had done to Tiffany in Minneapolis. I tried to be as specific as I could because any detail might matter, but when I had finished sharing and Mart and Mom had filled in the detail I'd missed from the story Tiffany told us at the steak house, Tuck still looked baffled.

"Well, that's just awful, but it actually makes Tiffany have motive in the murder more than it explains why someone would attack her," the sheriff said. Then, he raised his hand as if to stop the words that might come toward him. "Now, I'm not saying she is the murderer. I'm just saying that this information doesn't really help me solve this crime."

I let out a long breath. "Right. Sorry. That's all I know."

Mart and Mom nodded.

I sat back against the base of the couch and stared out the window over Cate's shoulder, hoping something would come to me. But Cate's sudden leap to her feet broke my train of thought.

"I just remembered something. Scott is from Minneapolis, too, isn't he?" she shouted.

"Scott? The hair dresser?" Stephen asked.

"THAT'S RIGHT," I said. "Maybe he knows something. I mean that kind of story would have been in the news, right? Maybe he knows things Tiffany didn't think to tell us?"

The sheriff took out his notebook. "This is the guy who owns the new salon on Main Street, right?"

"That's the one," Cate said. "He's a really nice guy and very good at his work." She pointed at her own hair and then at mine but frowned when my bandana sort of blunted her illustration. "I'm sure he would help if you ask him."

"Good thought. Thanks." The sheriff stood from the couch and helped Lu to her feet. "Well, this is helpful information. I'm still not sure how it all fits together, but we will figure it out," he said with a pointed look at me. "And by *we*, I mean the police."

I raised both hands over my head. "I have no desire to figure this one out, Sheriff." When he rolled his eyes, I said, "Well, I have the desire, but no intention of doing that. This one is all yours."

Tuck laughed. "Okay, then. Well, thanks for lunch. See you all around."

Mart helped Lu gather the ramekins and carry them to their car, but when she came back, she was frowning. "What?" I asked as she dropped to the floor and put her head on my shoulder.

"I just realized that we probably need to go tell Tiffany that the sheriff knows her story and that he's going to ask Scott about it." She sighed. "She said she was fine with us sharing, and I know she meant that. But it's only fair that we give her a heads up that other people have heard it, too."

Henri stood up and helped Bear to his feet. "Please assure her that we will keep her story in complete confidence. But also tell her that we're all here for her if she needs anything."

"Yes, please do," Walter added for himself and Stephen. "Thanks for lunch, Mama Beckett," he added as he bent to kiss Mom on the cheek.

Pickle handed me his card as he left. "If she needs me, tell her

I'm waiving my fee." He gave me a quick hug and headed out the door.

As Daniel, Mart, and I watched our friends leave, I felt a surge of joy at their kindness. Tiffany's story was definitely safe with them, but clearly, *she* wasn't safe until we figured out what in her story had made her a target.

IT WAS after one p.m. when I finally made it in to the shop, but Marcus and Rocky had the place running like a well-oiled machine. Marcus had even spruced up the pumpkin display to make it a bit more Thanksgiving-like, and it looked wonderful. Little gourds and squash had joined the pumpkins, and the books dealt with everything from recipes to Native American history to how to deal with family conflict at the holiday. The books were tastefully arranged, and I knew we'd be reordering a lot of titles soon.

The crowd from the festival was still enjoying a last afternoon in town, so sales were still brisk. I was especially thrilled to see that Galen and Mack had come back to pay a visit. I loved that guy. He always made me feel so good about my business, and when I felt good about my business, I felt good about myself.

Today he was shopping for mysteries that featured LGBTQ+ characters because he was preparing, already, for next June's Pride Month. He wanted to feature one book written by a member of the LGBTQ+ community or with a LGBTQ+ main character every day that month on his Instagram page. So he and I spent a couple of hours scouring the internet for lists of appropriate books, and when he left, he had all the titles we'd found and already stocked and had special ordered ten more. Now, he was sitting in the café reading a copy of *The Body in the Bookmobile* by Connie B. Dowell. It was one of my personal favorites, and it featured a bi character so it was a great fit for Galen's project.

That man was going to keep my business going single-handedly if he kept buying that many books at a time. I didn't mind.

Mart came by late in the afternoon. For obvious reasons, the winery was going to be closed for a while, so she'd spent the afternoon at the hospital with Tiffany. "She's okay," Mart said as she sat down on the stool behind the register with a huge pumpkin spice latte. "The doctors decided to keep her one more night under observation, but I honestly think they are just trying to give her some rest. Don't tell her insurance company though." Mart smiled thinly.

"Did you tell her about . . ." My voice trailed off. I didn't really want to say, "Did you tell her about the big meeting of all the people we love where we shared her most painful life experience?" but that's what I was thinking.

Mart nodded. "I did. I told her everyone who was there and gave her all their messages." She smelled the spicy goodness of her drink before continuing. "When I handed her Pickle's card and told her he was offering his services *pro bono*, she started to cry. At first I thought she was upset because of our violation of her privacy, but instead she said, 'I should have trusted people sooner. I was just so scared.'"

Tears sprang to my eyes, and I reached over to take Mart's hand. "Oh that's so hard. I know what it's like to carry around a painful experience because you're afraid to share it." I thought back to how painful my marriage had been when I lived in San Francisco and how no one, not even Mart, had known. "Well, then, I'm glad we told people for her."

"Me, too," Mart said. "She got nervous when I told her Tuck was going to talk to Scott, but not because she didn't want him to know, she said. More because she had hoped they could be friends since they had both lived near Minneapolis."

"I get that. The places I've lived have flavored my life, and I love meeting people who know that flavor. She understood why Tuck was going to talk to him, though, right?" I glanced back over my shoulder to see if any customers were waiting to check out behind me. All clear.

"Totally. She even wanted me to tell Tuck that she'd meet with Scott herself if he thought that would help." Mart stood and stretched. "I thought that was a good sign, that she wasn't so scared anymore."

I walked with Mart to the front door. "Thanks for the update, Mart. You headed home to rest?"

"Nah. I am tired, but I feel pretty restless. I'm going to put on my running clothes and jog out to the winery. Tuck gave the all-clear for us to begin clean-up." She leaned over to hug me. "He said the wine in the cellars was in good shape, but I just want to check."

"You have your phone on you?" I didn't want anyone I loved far away just now, but I couldn't very well keep Mart in the shop or at home. But if she had her phone, I could check in.

"Right here," she said, patting her back pocket. "I'll text you when I get to the winery and again when I leave, okay?"

"Thanks." I watched her walk down the sidewalk before taking a deep breath and spinning around to tend the shop. Marcus was ringing up an entire stack of The Foxfire Books for a gorgeous young man in patchwork shorts who carried a giant backpack. I couldn't imagine carrying all fourteen of those books on any kind of hike, but then I remembered how Cheryl Strayed had burned pages of the books she read and thought maybe this guy was looking forward to a year's worth of kindling. I kind of liked the image of him reading a chapter and then burning that chapter. It felt, well, very Foxfire.

I was still imagining him by his campfire when Tuck came in and silently pointed to the backroom. I glanced at Marcus, who raised his eyebrows but then gave me an assured nod that said he had it all under control.

I followed Tuck to the backroom, and as soon as the door clicked shut behind me, Tuck said, "How well do you know Scott?"

I studied Tuck's face and held off on the hair flip that I'd thought about giving as an answer. "He cut my hair once, and then I've seen him a couple of times here in town."

"So not well, then?"

"No, not well." I sat down at the table in the corner. "Why?" The sheriff's expression was somber, and I could feel a knot growing in my stomach.

He pulled out a chair across from me. "I talked to him today, and he claimed to have only a faint recollection of the news story. I guess that's possible, but Tiffany's case was the top news story for almost a week there. So I decided to do a little digging."

I swallowed hard. "Okay," I said quietly. "You found something?"

"Did Scott mention anything to you about being an athlete?" Tuck's voice suddenly took on the tone he used for police work, heavier and slower.

I pictured Scott's salon as I tried to remember our conversation, and I had a flash. "Yes, he was some sort of back-thing on a football team."

"A running back," Tuck said as he suppressed a smile. "Your knowledge of sports terminology is really quite remarkable, Harvey."

"Yes, that's it. He said he was fast, I think." I made a mental note to read a few sports books just to brush up on the terms. It's hard for me to remember things if I can't connect them to things I already know. I hoped this didn't mean I was going to have to actually watch a football game.

"Right. Running backs are the ones who catch the ball, and they have to be quite quick. Usually, they train as runners, some of them were even runners first." Tuck looked at me while I let that sink in.

I studied the sheriff's face and let his words process through my brain. "OOH," I said.

"There she is. Right. Yep, Scott was a runner . . . and he trained with Coach Cagle. I guess he didn't mention that."

"No, he most certainly did not . . . and we were talking about Coach Cagle directly. Actually, I remember him saying something about the "guy who was killed." At the time, it sounded like he just didn't know the guy, but now—"

"Now it sounds like he was trying to hide that he did know him." The worry lines on Tuck's face had gotten significantly deeper. "Alright, so was anyone else there while you two were talking."

"Yes," I practically shouted. "Cate was. Want me to call her?"

Tuck pulled his hand down his face. "I was trying so hard to keep you out of this investigation, but yes, I think I need you to call her."

I sighed and took out my phone, and within five minutes, Cate was sitting with us at the table. Tuck had prompted me not to tell Cate any details, just that we needed to talk to her about Cagle's murder, so I let Tuck lead the conversation.

He walked her through the same questions he'd asked me – how well did she know Scott? What did she know about his time in Minneapolis? Did she know he was a runner?

That last question was what tipped her off, and she gasped. "He knew Coach Cagle in Minneapolis!" She looked from Tuck to me. "Why didn't he tell us that? He acted like he didn't know him at all."

Tuck dropped his head back and looked at the ceiling. "So that confirms it. He was lying."

Cate looked at me, and I could see the panic in her eyes. The big connection had been laid bare, so I didn't think there was any harm in sharing what Tuck had told me. "He trained with Cagle . . . as a runner."

"What?!" She paused and looked into the middle distance. "Oh, because he's a running back. He needed speed training."

I dropped my head and turned my eyes up at my dear friend. "You knew that running backs got training in, well, running?"

"You didn't?" she asked with a laugh.

"Harvey is not up on sports, apparently," Tuck said, a tiny smile softening the worry in his face.

"Well, there's a difference between "not up on sports" and "oblivious," but that's a conversation for another day." Cate took a deep breath. "What are you going to do now?"

The sheriff folded his hands on the table. "I'm not sure, but I feel I'm missing something. There's some tie between the events of last night and Coach Cagle's murder, but I just can't get my hands on it."

I leaned back and stretched, hoping that a little more blood flow would help me tie those threads together for the sheriff. But I never could get anywhere just thinking. I had to talk things out, so I started to do just that. "Okay, so we know that Cagle and

Scott knew each other in Minneapolis, trained together in fact. And we know that Cagle trained Tiffany, too." I felt like one of those cartoon characters with a light bulb over their heads as I made the connection. "So do Tiffany and Scott know each other then?"

"Nope, not possible. Remember, they talked on Saturday, before the parade. It sure looked to me like they were meeting for the first time," Cate said.

I sighed. She was right. Neither of them had shown even a flicker of recognition. "Still, it's worth asking Tiffany, don't you think? Maybe she had one of those moments where his face looked familiar, but in a new setting, she couldn't place him. That happens to me all the time. I ran into this guy from Baltimore once on a random street in San Francisco, and even though he was calling my name, it took me a couple of minutes to place him."

Tuck stood up. "Harvey's right. We need to talk to Tiffany, but it's not urgent. She's coming home tomorrow. I'll talk to her then."

Cate and I stood, too, and I felt the lack of sleep and the overwhelm from the past days finally catching up to me. I looked at the clock on the wall – almost six o'clock. Good. Only an hour more to go before I could collapse on my couch with a chunk of cheese, some Ritz crackers, and *The Big Flower Fight* on Netflix. I needed some giant flower sculptures and no drama for one night.

As the three of us walked out, I noticed that the shop was mostly empty. The last tourists of the season had headed home, and we were back to the barebones of the neighborhood customers for the next few months. I would miss the extra income, but I was also looking forward to quieter days and more time with the people I loved.

Just as we were about to say good-bye to Tuck, Elle came in, and she was pulling a cart full of flowers. "I wanted to replace the ones in the box out front if you don't mind. The image of your blood and that knife against those plants – I just didn't want everyone to keep seeing that every day."

I stepped forward and hugged my friend. "You are too sweet. It's not necessary for my sake, but if you'd feel better, please replant away." I turned to Tuck. In the excitement of the past few hours, I'd pretty much lost track of what was happening with the knife, my sore fingers notwithstanding. "Any news on that?"

"Nope, not yet. Unlike on TV, the crime labs are closed on weekends." He winked at me. "I'll let you know what you need to know when I know it." Then he waved and headed out the front door.

Elle winked and said, "He gotcha."

I laughed and helped her wheel her cart back out to the sidewalk and install the plants before dusk came on. This time she'd brought mums, gorgeous orange ones with red and yellow stripes. She planted them close together, so the finished look was a solid, undulating band of color that looked amazing. I gave her a tight squeeze and giggled as she pulled her wagon down the street. All she needed were some pigtails to finish the picture of a little girl with her wagon.

A few minutes later, Mart came back.

"That was a short run," I snarked.

The blush on her cheeks told me something was up.

"I'm here to escort you home," she said as she swung a teetering pizza box from out behind her back, "with dinner."

The smell of melted cheese, fresh bread, and tomato sauce made me weak in the knees, but I got distracted from my hunger by the fact that I didn't recognize the pizza box. "Where did that come from?"

Mart blushed again, and I knew the answer. "Symeon is making pizza now?" I asked.

She smiled. "They just put in a pizza oven." After a long sigh, "the scent lured me in as I jogged by."

"I'm sure it was just the smell of pizza crust that drew you," I winked at her. "But really, a pizza oven at the French restaurant?" I couldn't see Max going for this plan.

"Apparently," Mart said, "they're morphing into more of a fusion European bistro vibe. I hear that manicotti is next on the list followed by Belgian fries."

I laid my hand over my heart. "You need to stop before I rush right over."

"Max is there." Mart said with a laugh.

"Alrighty then, urge to eat fries suppressed." I scanned the shop. It was empty except for Marcus who was closing out the register. "It'll just be a minute." I walked over to Marcus and nodded at the total. It *had* been a good day, a very good day.

We tucked the cash into the safe, signed out of the register, and did a last walk-through of the shop. Rocky turned off the lights in the café, and we turned off the neon OPEN sign before setting the alarm and closing up for the night. Rocky and Marcus headed toward his apartment over Daniel's garage, and Mart and I scooted in the other direction as fast as our tired feet could take us. Cold pizza is good, but nowhere near as good as fresh, hot, wood-fired pizza.

Once we were home, I grabbed a couple of cheap paper plates and paper towels, and we slid our legs under the coffee table and turned on the finale of *The Big Flower Fight*. Secretly, I was rooting for Jim and Ralph because I am a sucker for the under-dog, but I actually thought Henck and Yan would win.

We had just gotten to the final minutes of the competition when Mart's phone buzzed against the table. She glanced down, and then grabbed the remote to pause it. "It's Tiffany," she said.

I leaned back and waited as Mart replied before asking, "She okay?"

"Yeah. She's just wondering if I can pick her up from the hospital tomorrow. Feels like she needs a little moral support."

"Of course she does. You told her you'd be there? Can you be there?" I asked. I didn't think Mart had a consulting job for tomorrow, but sometimes she booked things last minute.

"Yep. I told her I'd be there at ten." Mart stretched. "I wish you could come. I think she could use a couple of shoulders just now."

She reached for the remote, but I grabbed it before she did. "One second."

I dialed Marcus' number, feeling a little guilt for interrupting his evening with Rocky but also thinking he deserved a phone call, not just another text to ask if he could cover for me. Within a minute, he had readily agreed to open – with me taking his closing shift – and said to tell Tiffany and Mart hello. "I'm in," I said as I handed Mart the remote, and we watched the floral victors be crowned.

13

The next morning, Mart and I walked into Tiffany's room with the most ridiculous pair of leggings we could find at the dollar store – neon yellow and green stripes and a matching neon yellow shirt. We figured she might not have anything to wear home, given that her clothes were probably in evidence, not to mention ruined. Plus, garish attire always lifts the mood when worn in jest.

As soon as we walked in, Tiffany started laughing because, of course, we couldn't let her be the only one in a ridiculous outfit. I had pulled a pair of parachute pants out of the back of my closet, and Mart had on pegged jeans and three pairs of socks in alternating colors. We were the worst of eighties fashion, including Mart's high pony that was tied up with a scrunchy. I felt absurd, but Tiffany's laugh was worth it.

She donned her leggings and T-shirt and thanked Mart profusely for the extra scrunchy we'd brought along. By the time she was discharged, the entire staff had been by to see us, and I could see the plans for an eighties day forming in the charge nurse's eyes. She looked like a woman who might be willing to rip the collar off a sweatshirt if her outfit required it.

We were just packing up the last of Tiffany's things when I heard the door to her room close. I turned around, expecting to see the on-call doctor or a nurse there, but instead, it was Scott . . . and this time, his tattoos didn't look charming. He looked downright menacing.

Instinctively, I stepped between him and Tiffany, and Mart slid over to put her arm around Tiffany's shoulders, where they stood on the other side of the bed. I hoped she was also reaching for the phone by the bed, but I couldn't spare the glance to find out. Scott was moving toward us quickly.

Without thinking, I put my arm out in front of me and pressed it against the huge man's chest. He basically just plowed me backwards like one of those weight things I've seen used in the training montages of movies with football elements. I stopped when the hospital bed bent my knees and made sit down, and my sudden drop in height must have startled Scott because he stopped too.

"What do you want?" Mart hissed from behind me.

"I want her to know what she did to me," Scott's voice was almost a growl.

I turned to look at Tiffany, and her eyes were as big as latte mugs. She clearly was as lost as I was.

"What I did to you? I just met you the other morning before the parade," Tiffany's voice was shaking. "I honestly have no idea what you're talking about."

Scott took another step forward and loomed over me. "Liar!"

Mart pulled Tiffany closer and said, "Scott, you need to leave. If you have something to discuss with Tiffany, you need to address that to her attorney."

· · ·

"Or take it up with Sheriff Tucker," I added. "Right now, you're threatening us, and you need to stop." I pushed my way to my feet and slid out from under Scott's hulking body.

Scott looked over at me and stepped back. "You need to watch yourself?" He jabbed a finger across the bed toward Tiffany.

"Go," I said, pushing Scott toward the door as best I could. He backed up a little, and at that moment, the door swung open. The charge nurse took one look at the situation and said, "Sir, I'm going to have to ask you to leave, or I will have to call security."

Scott stared at Tiffany for one last second and then spun toward the door, slamming into the nurse as he went.

"Call security," I said as I jogged around the bed to grab Tiffany. I pulled my phone out of my pocket as Mart and I sandwiched Tiffany's shaking body between us. "Tuck," I said, "we need you at the hospital. Now."

Security was at the room within a minute, and the charge nurse told him what she'd seen and asked us to explain what had happened before she came in. He made notes, and then when Tuck arrived a few minutes later, out of breath and looking very worried, the guard repeated what we'd told him. By then, Tiffany was calmer as she sat up in a chair in the corner of the room.

Tuck knelt beside her and asked how she was. "Okay, I guess. But I don't know what he's talking about. Really, I don't."

"I know. But this might help." He pulled a computer-printed photo from his breast pocket and handed it to her. "Do you recognize this man?"

A gasp burst from her lips when she saw the photo. "Yes, he was one of Cagle's cronies. Another woman accused him of rape, and he and Coach Cagle became buddies, claiming that both that woman and I had filed false statements."

I peered over Tiffany's shoulder and studied the picture. Something about the guy looked familiar. "Wait, that's Scott."

Tiffany's head spun toward me. "What?! No it's not."

"Yes, it is. Look at his face, his eyes and nose. He's thinner here, and he doesn't have tattoos, but that's him." I pointed toward the face in the photo.

Tiffany leaned closer and studied the man. "Holy crap, you're right." All the color drained from her face. "He followed me here, didn't he?"

Tuck stood up. "It appears that way, but I can't figure out why."

"I know why," Tiffany said as she pulled her knees up to her chest. "It's because I testified against him."

"What? Did he attack you?" Tuck asked, taking his notebook out of his pocket.

"No, but I was there when he threatened that other woman. We had joined a support group and gotten to know each other that way, sort of the opposite of what Scott and Cagle did. We connected over our trauma," she said quietly.

"And they connected over their rage," Tuck said.

"Right. Anyway, Scott, although he went by another name then. Gavin, I think, came into a meeting and promised to make her pay." Tiffany shuddered. "The other women were too scared to testify, but I couldn't let him get away with that."

"That was brave," I said.

Tiffany shrugged. "I almost lost my nerve because Cagle was in the courtroom, right behind this guy. That's how I realized they knew each other. But I made it through the testimony, and then I moved, right away."

"They must have stayed in touch, then, and Scott/Gavin moved here after Cagle did," Tuck said.

My mind was racing, but I could feel pieces starting to click into place. "So Scott wrote the threatening message and planted the bomb at the winery then?"

"It sure seems that way. Clearly, he still carries a lot of that rage around, and now he's directing it at RAINN." Tuck sighed. "And at you. I'm sorry I let the security detail go this morning. I'll make sure there's a patrol car at your house when you get home."

Tiffany stood up. "Thank you." She shrugged on her sweatshirt. "It's time to go. I can't let these people scare me anymore." She straightened her shoulders and walked out the door, leaving Mart and me to follow as her very willing entourage.

The ride to Tiffany's house was quiet, and I supposed my friends were thinking much of what I was – how had we missed that about Scott? He'd seemed so nice, so self-aware. But then, I had been charmed by his skills, and I wondered how many other women had been, too. I couldn't help but wonder what his wife knew. Did his children know their father threatened women? The idea made me so sad.

The patrol car was already parked outside of Tiffany's waterside bungalow when we arrived, and I recognized one of the deputies from the winery bombing. He gave a small wave as the three of us went up the walk to her house.

Inside, Tiffany's home was cute and charming with its beach theme. Her furniture was a cream-color that would never withstand our animals but here was pristine without feeling fussy. A deep blue throw was draped over the corner of a comfy-looking club chair, and the fireplace was filled with an array of candles in different sizes. "Clearly, you like lighthouses?" I said with a smile as I pointed at the shelves on either side of the fireplace that were filled with dozens and dozens of lighthouses.

"I do. Something about the idea of someone else keeping the light on for safety, I guess," she said with a little blush on her cheeks.

Mart dropped into the club chair. "I wish someone had done that for you, Tiffany. You know, back then . . . I mean, what if someone had been a lighthouse to warn you about Cagle?"

Tiffany sat on her couch and kicked one long, neon-yellow leg over the arm of the sofa. I joined her and slid my shoes off before sliding my feet under her thigh. "Don't you wish someone had warned you."

"Every day. But then, I'm not sure I would have listened. Everyone thinks it won't be them, right? And when I was in the thick of it, I thought I was going crazy. When I tried to describe what he was doing to me, how I felt in danger but that he wasn't physically violent, I felt foolish, like I was making a big deal out of nothing."

Mart leaned forward. "I know just what you mean. This one time in a club, I was dancing away, and this guy kept coming up to me and grabbing my shoulders as he bumped his hip against mine. Each time I moved away and found another spot in the crowd, but over and over again, he came to me. I was terrified by the time the night was over, but when I tried to describe why, I just couldn't put my finger on it."

Tiffany nodded. "Exactly. Somewhere along the way I absorbed this idea that my discomfort or fear didn't matter unless I was actually in physical danger. But that's horse hockey. Danger is danger. Unsafe is unsafe, even if it's not physical." Her voice was adamant now, strong.

"Exactly," I said. "That's why I like the work that RAINN does on education. It teaches people to trust our instincts. If something feels unsafe, it *is* unsafe to us, and it's okay to leave that situation just because we feel that way." I don't think I had ever articulated that sentiment before, but now, I knew I needed to believe it. For myself, but for other women, too.

Mart leaned back and then cracked her knuckles. "Agreed. But we do need to discuss something serious." Tiffany and I looked each other and then back at her. "Horse hockey? Who says that?"

We all cracked up, and some of the fear and tension of the morning eased away. I wanted to stay and watch ridiculous movies with my two friends, but I had a business to run. So I left them as they began a *Bring It On!* marathon and drove to work. Mart had already arranged with Henri to get a lift home later in the day, and if I knew Henri, that lift home would entail her continued presence at Tiffany's house while her wonderful husband drove Mart to our house. I expected Tiffany would have constant company for the next few days if she wanted it. Our friends were good like that.

When I got to the shop just before noon, I was delighted to see Walter and Stephen sitting in the café, and again I wished I could sit down and chat with them. But I had left Marcus on his own enough for the past few days, so I simply waved to my friends and headed to the register.

Marcus was having a light-hearted but intense conversation with a middle-aged black man about which book about racial justice was most important. As I checked on our supply of bags and small bills, I listened to the two debate *The New Jim Crow* and *Just Mercy* as two alternatives. I had loved and been profoundly challenged by both books and made sure we always had them in the store. Still, I was at a total loss for words when Marcus said, "Which would you choose?" and looked at me.

I stared from one man to the other and found them both waiting patiently for my answer. "Um, well, I expect you might know better than I do," I said candidly.

The other man laughed. "Well, I expect we might have lived closer to what those authors describe, but maybe you're the better judge of which has more of an impact?"

I smiled. "Because I'm white, and we white people are responsible for making the changes to the system we created." It wasn't a question. Just a statement.

"Exactly," the man said.

I took a deep breath and thought about both books, about how each of them had changed me when I'd listened to them as I'd gone to and from work in San Francisco. "I'm going to say *Just Mercy*, but only because of the way Stevenson wrote it, not because the content was any more or less important than Alexander's work."

"You mean because he tells Johnny D's story?" Marcus asked.

"Exactly . . . and his own. Alexander's book is great for a book club discussion, but I happen to believe people get changed most by stories." I felt a little nervous about my choice, not wanting to disrespect either man's choice.

But Marcus smiled, and the other man reached out his hand to shake mine. "That is a good answer, Ms. Beckett. Now, do you have a few minutes to discuss hosting a Racial Justice Book Group here? I'm Wally Mick, head of the local NAACP chapter."

I grinned. "Nice to meet you, Mr. Mick, and yep, let's talk. I'd love to host your group. We need all the justice we can get." He and I headed back to the fiction section to work out logistics, and I felt more of the tension of the past few days fade away. This was just the sort of thing I hoped would happen in my store, especially given its history as an African American-owned gas station back in the days of Jim Crow.

Mr. Mick and I were just finishing up the plans for our first book club meeting in November when I heard the bell ring at the front door and then a commotion rising up there. "Better let you get back to it," Wally said as he stood and shook my hand. "See you in a couple of weeks."

I nodded and then walked as briskly as I could to the front door. There, Marcus was standing chest to chest with Scott, and while my assistant manager was neither tiny nor timid, he was clearly losing ground to the large hairdresser. I quickly dialed 911, told the dispatcher to send someone to the store immediately, and then walked up to stand beside Marcus. I was significantly shorter than he was, but I hoped that two us looked intimidating enough to get Scott to back off. I wasn't sure what he was upset about now, but I could guess.

"What's going on here?" I asked, squaring my shoulders and lifting my chin.

"I want to talk to Tiffany. I haven't been able to figure out where she lives, but I know you know. So tell me." Scott's eyes were wide, and he looked a little crazed.

Behind me, I could hear rustling, but I didn't dare turn my head away from Scott, even for a second. "I'm not telling you where Tiffany lives, Scott. You need to stop harassing her, and you need to leave." My voice was shaking, but I couldn't tell if it was from fear or from rage.

The bell rang over the door, and I saw my mom and dad walk in . . . Dad, sizing up the situation quickly, sent Mom back out, presumably to wait for help, and stepped around Scott to stand beside me. "Can I help you with something?" Dad's voice had the air of CEO that he used to use when he ran stockholder meetings. I'd attended a few of those meetings over the years as part of school projects, and I was always awed by my dad's command of a room. He wasn't intimidating, but he definitely knew how to command a room.

Scott took a step back. "Who are you?" He physically backed off, but his voice was just as angry.

"I think the better question is, who are you, and why are you here?" Dad leaned forward just a little and lorded his six-foot-four frame over Scott.

"I CAME to get some information from her," he stabbed the air near my face, and I felt my father shift his shoulder in front of mine. "But she's refusing to cooperate."

"Last I heard in this country, no one is required to share any information that they'd rather not . . . unless you are some sort of attorney or law enforcement officer with a warrant. Are you?" Dad's voice was quiet now, but somehow, that made it all the more ominous.

Scott's face went purple with rage. "Fine, but your posse can't protect you all the time," he spat as he spun and headed out the door.

Mom waited quietly as he passed her on the sidewalk, wise enough not to draw attention to herself, before she came in and said Tuck was thirty seconds away. "Look, there he is."

I stepped out to his car and pointed up the street toward Scott's salon. He took off at a jog as he shouted, "Close the store and lock the door."

When I walked back in, I saw a gathering of people near the front door and realized that all these people, including Mr. Mick, had witnessed that interchange. "I'm so sorry, everyone. I wish you hadn't had to see that."

Then, Stephen said, "Are you kidding? You were incredible." He pointed at Marcus, Dad, and me. "That guy was nuts to take on the three of you." The crowd behind him and Walter started to clap and cheer, and I realized that the sound I'd heard behind me was all these people literally having my back. Tears stung my eyes.

I looked at Marcus, who shrugged and smiled and then at Dad, who looked like he'd just scared away a bumble bee. Meanwhile, I felt like I'd been holding off a ballistic missile. My hands were shaking, and I felt a little faint. But to have the support of my community, not to mention witnesses to Scott's anger, that felt amazing.

Still, I hoped Tuck caught him. St. Marin's wasn't that big a town, and it wouldn't take Scott long to track Tiffany down if he was determined. I suddenly realized I had to warn Tiffany and grabbed my phone. Mart was still there, so I called her first. She said she and Tiffany would lock the house down after telling the officer on duty what had happened, just in case Tuck hadn't been able to get in touch with him yet. I told them I was sending reinforcements.

Then, I called Henri. She and Bear, who was off from the hospital for the day, were heading straight over. They were calling Pickle, too.

"What do you need now, Harvey?" Stephen asked as he slid up beside me and pulled me close. Walter looked at me with soft eyes.

I felt foolish, but I said, "I need Daniel."

"On it," Walter said as he headed for the door. "I'll run to get him and fill him in. An urgent "get to the bookstore" text might be too much." He jogged out the door.

"What else?" Stephen said.

With a flash, I remembered that Tuck had told me to close the store, so I asked Stephen to help me send people home with the promise of a ten percent discount if they came back later in the week. Within a couple of minutes, he and Rocky had gathered the stacks of books that people were considering, labeled them with the customer's name, and promised to hold them until the weekend in case someone wanted to come back for them. Then Stephen flipped off the neon sign and locked the door. He put a chair beside it and took up his self-appointed charge as doorman.

I saw Daniel and Walter jogging up the sidewalk with Taco lumbering along behind them. That Basset could hustle when need be. Stephen opened the door, and Daniel rushed over and hugged me. Then, he stood back and said, "Where is he?"

His face was calm, but there was a flint in his eyes that told me he was angry as all get out. "Tuck went after him."

Daniel took a deep breath. "Maybe I should go back him up?"

Walter walked over and put his hand on Daniel's forearm. "I think the sheriff has all the back-up he needs available. Besides, it might be wise to stay near Harvey at this point, right?"

I gave Walter a grateful smile. The idea of Daniel chasing after that crazed man made my blood ice over, and I really didn't want him to leave me. Not now. I needed his calm presence . . . that is if he could get calm.

Rocky walked over with a large mug and said, "Vanilla steamer. It'll calm you." Walter spun the comfy chair from the mystery section so that it faced the front door, and I lowered myself into it.

The smell of the vanilla helped soothe my nerves almost imme-diately, and the hot milk flushed some of the tension out of my neck, too. "Thank you, Rocky."

She nodded, and then she and Marcus pulled the wing chairs from fiction over and sat down near me. Daniel carried the stool from the behind the register, and Walter sat down on the floor against Stephen's knees. Apparently, no one was leaving, and I was grateful.

I checked in with Mart, and she said they were fine – the police officer was still there, and Henri, Bear, and Pickle had all arrived. They'd just ordered pizza and were going to watch *Schitt's Creek* to keep their mind off things. I thought that sounded amazing, especially the pizza.

Just then, Lu appeared at the front door, and when Stephen opened it for her, the smell of fresh tortillas, garlic, and chili wafted through the air, erasing all memory of my pizza craving. "Tuck said you were holed up here. I thought you might need snacks."

"Oh, Lu, thank you. Yes, please," I said as Marcus helped Lu clear the counter by the register. She quickly set up a buffet line for tacos and helped me up to get a plate. I was surprised I was hungry, but I couldn't possibly resist Lu's spicy black beans, queso, guacamole, and fresh salsa. I made myself two veggie tacos and went back to my chair.

I had just started on my second taco when Elle appeared at the door with her arms full of flowers. She looked puzzled, and I realized she was doing her usual Sunday afternoon flower delivery. Stephen opened the door, and she immediately set the flowers in his arms and came to me.

"What happened?" I explained the scene with Scott, and Elle groaned. "That nerve of that man."

I nodded. "But Lu has fortified us with fresh food. Help yourself." I sat back down and made quick work of my taco as Elle pulled a chair from the café and enjoyed her own.

That explanation followed by dinner happened twice more, first when Cate and Lucas arrived after Daniel texted Lucas to tell him what happened and then again when Woody got the news from Henri. Soon enough, everything but a single spoonful of guacamole was gone, and I tidied up that last sliver of yumminess.

Then, the heavy silence descended, and I began to wonder what was taking Tuck so long. I had thought he'd have let us know when he had Scott in custody, but maybe he was going to question him first before getting back to us. I couldn't just sit there waiting, so I got up and began to tidy the store. Marcus joined me, but soon, everything was in place . . . and my nerves started to jangle again.

"Let's face the shelves," Marcus said with a look of concern at my shaking hands. "We haven't done that in a while, and with all of us helping, we'll have the store looking perfect in no time."

I smiled. "Great idea," I said and meant it. Sometimes, the simplest things – like making sure all the book spines are lined up at the front edge of the book shelf – are the best medicine. So the team, all except Stephen who stayed at his post by the door, spread out after Marcus had demonstrated how to neatly arrange the books perfectly. Within a few minutes, the shelves were more perfect than they'd been when we opened, and I was feeling more relaxed, too, well, as relaxed as I could be until I found out what Tuck had learned from Scott.

I had just taken my seat again when Tuck appeared at the front door. Stephen let him in and immediately pulled his chair over by me so Tuck could sit down. The sheriff looked wan, and he was out of breath. I had never seen him out of breath. He didn't make a big deal out of it, but I knew Tuck spent an hour or two a day at the gym staying in shape for his job.

Rocky rushed over with a glass of ice water, and Lu pulled a café chair up and sat next to her husband as he caught his breath. After he pulled back the water in one long swig, he sighed and said, "We couldn't find him."

My heart sprang up into my throat. "Oh no," I whispered.

"How is that possible?" my dad asked from behind my chair. Mom appeared beside me and put her hand on my shoulder. My parents hadn't always been the most supportive of me, but they were making up for lost time now. "He had just gone down the street when you arrived," Dad continued.

"I don't know." Tuck looked mortified. "We scoured the streets, checked his home and shop, and put out an APB. But nothing. He's disappeared."

Daniel frowned as he said. "He's not exactly unobtrusive what with the huge muscles and the tattoos."

"Exactly," Tuck said. "He's intentionally hiding, which makes me nervous."

I swallowed hard. "We need to get to Tiffany." I knew our friend had people there, and I knew the officer was keeping a careful eye. But I also knew, with some sort of deep dread, that people and one police officer were not enough. "I'm going." I stood up.

Tuck said, "Okay" and headed toward the front door with me.

"Okay?!" Dad stormed forward, blocking our path. "Why would you let her go to where a killer might?" His face was bright red with anger and, I suspected, fear.

"Mr. Beckett, we don't know where Scott is. He could be coming back here, for all I know. So I think it's safer for everyone to be in one location where my deputies and I can keep them safe." The sheriff pointed to everyone in the room. "Caravan over?"

My friends and parents didn't even hesitate. They grabbed their bags and helped turn out the lights. Daniel and I set the alarm and locked the door, and then we were all in various vehicles and headed toward Tiffany.

I texted Mart, "The cavalry is on the way" with a little horse emoji. I expected her to reply right back with something snarky, but nothing. Not even the three little dots to say she was typing. I hoped she had just set her phone aside while they watched TV, but I doubted it. I leaned forward from the back of my parents' car and said, "Dad, go faster."

He caught my eye in the rearview mirror, gave a quick nod, and dropped the pedal to the floor. I called Tuck as we sped around his patrol car. "Mart's not answering."

"Got it. I'm dispatching cars now." Then he raced back around us and led the way. I texted Stephen and Walter who had Elle and Woody with them and then Marcus and Rocky, who were bringing up the rear with Cate and Lucas and told them to be safe but that we were going as fast as we could.

Rocky's single word text was, "Praying," and while I wasn't much of a pray-er myself, I was grateful. I sat back in my seat and watched Tuck's taillights as he whipped toward Tiffany's house. I hoped we weren't too late.

When we pulled up, the patrol car was still out front, and the officer was standing beside his door. He looked calm, and I felt my shoulders relax a bit. I burst out of the car as soon as Dad stopped and ran toward Tuck was had parked just beside his deputy with his car blocking the street. "Everything's okay, then?" I shouted as I ran up.

The deputy looked from Tuck to me and back. "No problems here. I heard your radio dispatch, though. You think he's coming here?"

Tuck nodded. "Help me get everyone set up as they arrive," he told the deputy, who nodded and stepped around Tuck's car as the first of the additional officers arrived.

"Can I go in? I still haven't heard from Mart," I asked, my voice a bit squeaky with fear.

"Let me go first," Tuck said and put his hand on his gun at his hip.

I followed right behind him, too eager to be sure my friends were okay to actually be cautious myself. I could hear footsteps behind me and saw Daniel then Dad and finally my mom lined up like we were queuing for ice cream at the local Dairy Freeze. I had to suppress a giggle as I imagined us as a breach team from one of those Navy SEAL TV shows. Tuck was the leader, and Daniel was the muscle. Dad was the language expert, and Mom was the sharp shooter. I wasn't sure exactly what that made me, but if Mart was in trouble, I'd be whatever I needed to be to keep her safe. I wished I'd thought to grab something from Dad's car to use as a weapon, but I wasn't sure how effective a travel umbrella might be in a fight.

Tuck led us around the back of the house, which maybe should have tipped me off to his concerns. At the time, though, I was just so eager to check on Mart that I didn't even think about it. He kept his head down below the windows and gestured for us to do the same. That tiny motion of his hand woke me up to what was happening, and I realized we were the breach team. Panic started to climb my skin.

Part of my brain was trying to work out why Tuck would let us do something like this. I knew it probably wasn't wise to let four civilians storm the castle, so to speak, but I'd long ago learned that Tuck knew what he was doing. And if he thought it was better for us to go in than his armed and trained deputies, I had to trust him.

At that moment, we climbed the small back stoop, and Tuck

gestured me forward. He put his lips right to my ear and said, "I want you to go in like everything is completely fine. Try to smile if you can." Then he reached down and ripped a handful of mum stems off the potted plant Tiffany had by her back door. "Take these."

I stared at the flowers for a minute and then nodded. I knocked quickly and then went on in, like it was a normal day when an enraged man was holding my friends hostage. For a split second when the door opened, I did think everything was fine, and I smiled. "I brought you flowers," I said to Tiffany, who was seated in the club chair closest to the TV.

That's when I noticed the terror in her eyes.

14

I hoped my smile hadn't faltered too much as I relifted the corners of my mouth while also trying to telepathically communicate to Tiffany then to Mart that help was behind me. Mart darted her eyes quickly to the corner of the room that I couldn't yet see. So Scott was there. I let out a long slow breath, hoping he couldn't see me either, and turned back into the kitchen.

"I brought you some flowers from Elle," I stressed Elle's name a bit. Maybe Mart would pick up on the fact that our friends were here. "I'll just put them in water." I walked the few feet to the the sink and reached for the cabinet above the sink. I took two glasses out of the cabinet and turned the water on to fill one glass while I set the other in the window sill and shaped my fingers like a gun against the glass as I did. I could only hope Tuck saw and was preparing. Then, I spun back toward the living room, took a deep breath, and walked in with the glass full of flowers.

I tried to keep my eyes trained on Tiffany as she sat in the club chair, like I was just bringing her flowers. Then, I turned my back – bracing myself – toward the corner where I thought Scott was hiding as I spoke to Mart. "You would not believe how busy we were today." I leaned in and gave her hug as I whispered against her ear. "Help is here."

Then I turned to hug Henri next to her, shake Bear's hand a bit further around the room toward Scott, and finally to Pickle, who was by the front door, just far enough away from the corner that I could still, I hoped, feign that I didn't know Scott was there. I took yet another deep breath and dropped onto the couch between Mart and Henri, and only then did I look up and throw on my most surprised face when I saw Scott in the corner, a pistol aimed at Tiffany's head.

I let out the most pitiful squeak in the history of performances as Scott looked at me and said, "Hello Harvey."

"Um, what are you doing?" I said, acting like the dumb woman Scott apparently thought all of us were.

He glowered at me. "You thought I wouldn't find her."

At this point, I could only hope that I'd bought Tuck enough time to prepare because I was done pretending. "I'm not that dumb, Scott. St. Marin's is a small place. I figured it was only a matter of time." I stretched my arms over my head in my best semblance of nonchalance. "You thought I'd come here alone."

Just then, both the front and the back doors flew open, and I hit the floor. I couldn't lift my head to look around, but in the direction I'd landed, I could see that Henri, Bear and Pickle had followed my lead.

A shot rang out across the room, and I heard a thud. I squeezed my eyes shut, not ready to see who had been hit. That's when I got kicked in the face.

When I came to a few minutes later, my mom was standing over me and saying, "We're going to have to take her to see that concussion doctor. You know, the one Will Smith played in that movie."

I blinked my eyes, and someone whipped a flashlight past my eyes. "She's awake," a woman said, and I squinted just enough to make out one of the EMTs from Saturday night checking the pulse in my right arm.

"Harvey!" Mom lunged forward to hug me, but the EMT threw up an arm and stopped the attack.

"Maybe give her a moment," the woman said. "She did just take a steel-toed boot to the temple."

I groaned. "Is that what it was? That jerk kicked me?"

"Actually, no, this jerk did." Tuck was standing at my feet and looking at me as I lay in a gurney on an ambulance. "I'm sorry, Harvey. He caught me off guard when he thrashed, and I lost my footing."

I couldn't help but chuckle. "So this is the thanks I get for staying out of your investigation and then leading the charge into the battle zone."

The sheriff rolled his eyes. "You weren't infiltrating a terrorist stronghold in Kabul, Harvey." He squeezed my foot. "But thank you. Your signal with the gun and the glass was just the information we needed."

I smiled. "I wasn't sure you'd get it. But I had to act fast."

"It made perfect sense. The gun, of course, but also the glass – the situation was fragile. Well-done." Tuck patted my ankle. "I'll need your statement later, but first, let's be sure you're okay."

Mom looked at Dad and said, "See? All those years of charades paid off."

It was Dad's turn to roll his eyes then.

A FEW MINUTES LATER, the EMT said I was good to go. I didn't have a concussion, as best she could tell, but someone should stay with me and wake me every two hours just to be sure. She looked at my mother, and Mom practically raised her hand to volunteer.

I stifled yet another groan. My mother had never been the super nurturing type, but she was stellar at being useful. And if useful included waking her exhausted daughter to be sure she was conscious, Mom was in. It was going to be a long night after an already long night.

I climbed gingerly out of the ambulance as I waited for my vision to un-double, and then I looked around. Mart and Tiffany were talking to one deputy, and Henri, Bear, and Pickle were giving their statements to another. Daniel, Elle, and Woody were sitting on the curb in front of Tiffany's house with hot cups of coffee, and when Elle saw me headed that way, she reached behind her and brought out another cup.

"Oh, thank God." I winced. "It is decaf, though, right?" I already had Mommy Dearest eager to wake me up. I didn't need to have trouble falling asleep, too.

"Of course," Elle said. "We women of a certain age need to guard each other's sleep." She winked at me and then put her fingertips against my temple. "You are going to have a really nice shiner there."

I smiled. I'd had a black eye once before, and while I didn't relish the pain, the attention had been pretty fun. I turned to Daniel, "Will you still love me if I look like Rocky Balboa after he lost?"

He gently pulled me to his chest. "Of course. As long as you don't start calling me Adrian."

I shook my head. "As long as you don't call me Rocky. One is enough."

"Speaking of which," Woody said, "They both said to tell you they've got the store tomorrow. You are to stay home." Our friend the woodsmith was typically pretty soft-spoken and passive, but there was a tone to his voice that told me he wasn't simply the messenger here. I had a feeling that if I showed up in the bookstore tomorrow, I might be contending with a wiry older man at the door.

"You don't have to convince me. I am so tired I can barely stand." I leaned harder into Daniel's chest. "Take me home?"

Daniel grinned. "I'm afraid we must rely on your parents for that honor. Remember?"

I sighed. Right, we hadn't brought either of our vehicles. "Fine. But Mom, you drive. My head can't take any of Dad's action movie moves."

Dad grinned. "They were pretty great, huh? I wonder if Matt Damon needs a stunt driver."

"Matt Damon, Mr. B," Daniel said. "Isn't he a bit too, well, youthful? Maybe Robert Redford."

I glanced from Daniel to my dad and wondered exactly when they'd become friendly enough to tease each other. I liked it.

When we got back to our house, Mart and I immediately changed into pajamas, and Mom set us up with hot chocolate and Moose Tracks ice cream, a personal favorite combination, while Dad laid a fire and Daniel took care of the dogs and Aslan. Mayhem and Taco were a bit on edge, sensing the stress among their people, but the cat, well, she was just put out that someone was taking her seat again. I took pity on her and laid her chenille throw out beside the fireplace, and she looked at me with a bit less disdain after that.

Daniel played with my hair as I stretched across the couch, and Mart rested in the pallet of blankets that Mom made for her on the floor. She'd always done that for me when I was sick, and for whatever reason, it had been the best place in the world to recover. Mart seemed to be liking it, too, but her smile really brightened when a certain red-headed chef appeared at the door with personal ramekins of Creme Brulee.

"You're not at the restaurant tonight?" she asked as she spread out the blanket beside her.

"I asked for the night off. I wanted to be here." He blushed, but he didn't look away from her. "I'm so sorry that happened."

She put her hand in his as they lay side by side and watched the first episode of *Kim's Convenience* with us all. It was maybe the weirdest and sweetest first date ever.

Eventually, though, we had all laughed enough to displace a little of the terror of the day, and people began to trickle out. I sent Mom home, despite her protests about her promise to the doctor and the obvious glee she was feeling about waking me up repeatedly. Daniel stayed and helped me clean up while Mart walked Symeon to the door. We tried not to spy, but in an open-concept house, everything is in view, even a tiny, gentle first kiss.

I was happy for my friend . . . I was also still terrified. Daniel offered to stay on the couch, just for reassurance, but Mart and I nixed that idea, told him we'd keep our phones by the bed, and climbed into my bed side-by-side, like it was a slumber party, not the night after a near-death experience.

We stayed up talking for a while, mostly about first kisses and our high school boyfriends and haircuts. I had rocked an asymmetrical cut back then, too, but I'd also used a lot of gel. I couldn't say I'd been quite on the cusp of fashion, but at least I hadn't done the great flip-up and flip-down of bangs that Mart had apparently sported.

Eventually, we fell asleep, our hands touching for comfort. More than ever I was grateful for my friend.

The next morning, I woke early, texted Marcus to thank him for covering the store for me, again, and began planning my new window display about sexual assault. It was a little heavy for the holidays, but it felt right, too. Plus, the other window was already chock-full of pumpkin and cranberry cheerfulness, thanks to Marcus. A little reality in the midst of all the holiday frenzy might be just what we needed.

Besides, I needed to do something, anything, to help bring about change. A window display or a book club wasn't much, but it was something. And in my world that was so much formed by books, it was a big something to me.

So when I couldn't simply sit around the house any longer, I tied a bandana around my hair, leashed up Mayhem, and walked into town. Then, quietly, I took down the pumpkin display that Marcus hadn't yet changed over to Thanksgiving and did my new one. Right in the middle, I dangled purple letters I had cut out from poster board. They said, "We believe you."

Then, I prominently featured Ellen Bass's classic *The Courage To Heal*, and then I added in *Speaking Truth to Power* by Anita Hill and marveled at how, as a child, I'd absorbed the narrative that made it so easy for me to believe she was making it all up. I put in as many other titles as I could, including *We Believe You* by Annie E. Clark and Andrea L. Pino and then, because everything Roxane Gay does is magical, I put the final pièce de résistance – her book *Not That Bad*.

When I stepped back, the display was a tender show of solidarity for victims. I knew it wouldn't suit everyone, and I expected I'd get a few complaints from those whose political leanings encouraged them toward a different viewpoint. But I didn't care. For me, this wasn't about political parties. It was about human rights, and I would never feel bad about that.

15

That evening, all our friends gathered at Stephen and Walter's waterside house. This promised to be one of the last mild evenings until Spring, and so we took full advantage of their large deck, the bonfire on the grass by the water, and a widely disparate assortment of hot dog roasting sticks. Daniel claimed that his stick only produced burnt hot dogs, and mine seemed determined to keep mine lukewarm . . . so he ate the one I cooked, and I ate his, which was perfectly charred and tasted amazing in a potato bun with ketchup and relish.

Everyone had come with something to add – potato chips, coleslaw, some sort of chili that Lu swore was the only thing that made hot dogs palatable. Lucas even whipped up a batch of pumpkin cupcakes with cream cheese frosting for the gathering. It was perfect, especially when Stephen and Walter revealed their brand new bar that rivaled the best liquor stores on the Eastern Shore.

After everyone had eaten their fill and settled in by the fire with a cupcake and some of the most amazing hot toddies I'd ever had, Tuck filled us in on the full story. Mart sat between Symeon, whose weekly night off was Tuesday, and Tiffany and held both of their hands tightly. I kept a close eye on Tiffany, and it seemed like she slowly relaxed as Tuck talked. Maybe that was what closure looked like.

Apparently, Scott and Coach Cagle knew each other, just as Tiffany had suspected, but what she didn't know was that they had met online in a chat room for men who claimed they'd been falsely accused of sexual assault. "It was the most misogynistic thing I've ever seen," Tuck said. "I had to confirm the story the detective from Minneapolis told me about how Cagle and Scott knew each other, but I could barely stand to be there. It was so disgusting."

Lu leaned against her husband. "Good. I'm glad it disgusts you. If it didn't, I'd be worried." Every woman around the fire nodded.

"Eventually, the men decided to meet up in person, and apparently they not only became friends but they also committed two 'alleged,'" Tuck made air quotes, "rapes, too. But they both skipped town before they could be prosecuted. The prosecutors had them dead to rights for those two attacks, but they couldn't find them, so the crimes are still unsolved."

I slid closer to Daniel, whose jaw was clenched so tightly that I thought he might crack a molar. I ran my fingers along his jaw. "It's okay. Tuck's not finished with the story," I said quietly. "Right, you're not finished?"

"No," he smiled at me. "Gavin – Scott as you knew him – is being extradited back to Minnesota to stand trial for those two rapes as soon as he finishes his trial here. He's still claiming innocence of any sexual assault, but he has admitted to the threats and the bombing on the grounds that he was simply defending himself."

"Defending himself," Mart sputtered. "In what way is that possible?"

"It won't stand up in court," Tuck said. "But he's claiming that his reputation was sullied because the women he attacked were willing—"

"Okay, we get it," Cate said as she looked at Tiffany. "We don't need to hear more of that BS do we?"

"Definitely not," Tiffany said. "But he will stand trial?"

"He will. Twice, and both the attorney general here and the one in Minnesota assure me that he will be put away for the rest of his life." Tuck took a long pull from his beer. "As he should.""Amen," Bear whispered. "But what's the story with Cagle's death? Did you figure out who committed that crime?"

Tuck grinned. "Actually, that was pretty easy. Scott, I mean Gavin did it. He was afraid Cagle was going to go back to Minnesota and rat him out, so he took care of the threat. That, it seems, is the reason he came here." He looked at Tiffany. "I really think he had no idea you were here, no clue that Cagle had stalked you here. But when he found out—"

"Then, I was a threat, too." Tiffany's voice was matter-of-fact. "Well, that clears that up."

Mart put her arm around Tiffany's shoulder. "You okay?"

"I think so. I mean, maybe. Okay, probably not, but I do feel relieved. No matter how much I know none of this was my fault, it's hard not to believe that on some level when everyone tells you it is." She took a long, deep breath. "But this proves none of this was my responsibility."

All at once, Henri, Mart, Cate, and I stood up and knelt by Tiffany's feet. "This is not your fault. None of it. No matter what anyone says," I said. I looked in Tiffany's face and saw tears spilling down her cheeks. "We will tell you that over and over again for as long as you need the reminder." Then, we all hugged her until we fell into a giggling, crying heap in the grass.

. . .

THE NEXT MORNING in the shop, I was just settling in with my vanilla latte so I could run the previous week's sales figures. Rocky was bouncing along to Lizzo in the café, and I was marveling at the speed with which that woman could spit out words. It was feeling like it was going to be a great day.

Just then, the bell over the door rang and two women walked in. One woman was African American with long dark hair spilling down her back, and the other woman was white, her graying hair cropped close to her head. They were both gorgeous, and I was excited to see new faces . . . until their eyes met mine.

Usually, when customers first step into the shop, they look around, get a lay of the land, so to speak. But these two women scanned just long enough to find me at the register and made a beeline. Typically that kind of focus on the person in charge precedes a complaint, so I braced myself.

But when they reached the counter, the white woman put her hand on mine, and the other woman leaned over the counter to hug me. "We saw your window display on Galen's Instagram, and we came down right away from Baltimore. We wanted to thank you in person."

"Thank you," the other woman said. "You have no idea—" She tilted her head and looked at my face. "Well, maybe you do know just how much that means. Thank you."

"Now, where do I get one of those delicious smelling drinks," her friend asked.

Rocky shouted over her music. "In here, ladies. I'll hook you right up."

The two women waved and headed to the back just as I heard

the bell ring over the door again. I wiped the tears from my eyes and turned to greet the person who had just come in.

Quickly, though, my attempt to hold back my tears became futile because there was Daniel with a huge bouquet of flowers and a small sign that read, "I'll always believe you. Always."

I smiled and tried to contain my sobs, and then he turned the card over. "Will you marry me?" it said.

I nodded, and then I saw a happy tear slide down his cheek. The cheers from the café drowned out even Lizzo.

NATIONAL SEXUAL ASSAULT
TELEPHONE HOTLINE

800-656-HOPE

or Chat with a Live Person at RAINN.org

TOME TO TOMB

My memories of Santa Claus are scant. For a few years when I was little, extra toys appeared on Christmas morning, and a couple of times, the cookies got eaten, too. I expect Mom and Dad took me to the mall or some such place to sit on the guy in the red suit's lap, too. But my most vivid memory associated with Santa was finding my presents from Santa in my grandfather's car one December. The magic ended there. . . at least as far as Santa was concerned.

But I've always loved Christmas. As a kid, I loved the church Christmas pageants and the Midnight Candlelight service on Christmas eve. I adored driving around and looking at the lights on all the houses, and the Grinch always made an appearance on an evening when I got to stay up late and watch TV in my pajamas with a big, marshmallow-laden cup of hot cocoa. But by far, my favorite part of Christmas was the people. Mom always had charity parties at our house, and Dad made sure his firm had a kid-friendly holiday gathering. I loved them all, even though I often sat in the corner and dipped in and out of my current book while people swirled around me. I was introverted as a kid, but I was also a lover of people, at least people watching.

Which is why when I learned that St. Mariners had been without their decades-long tradition of having Santa greet children on Main Street, I agreed to host. Santa had been absent last year, and while I hadn't known why our little business district had felt a bit wan, it now was clear that Santa's absence was the cause. Apparently, the Chamber of Commerce had always set up Santa's cottage in the old gas station that was now my bookstore, but they'd felt awkward about asking me if they could use the space when I'd taken it over a little over a year back. And apparently, the town couldn't quite figure out what to do instead, so no Santa.

This year, though, an entire front corner of the bookstore was going to be Santa's workshop this year, and he would be on-hand every weekend in December to greet our youngest (and our most fun-loving older) guests and hear their Christmas wishes.

The trouble was that my staff and I were in a stalemate over what we should call the space where Santa would be. My assistant manager, Marcus, wanted to call it the Santa Zone because, as he said, it would be a tip of the hat to Fro-zone, his favorite character from *The Incredibles* movies. I liked that idea, especially because our Santa was going to be black, like the character voiced by Samuel L. Jackson in the movies, but it also reminded me of some sort of sports / arcade / game complex, and I really didn't want to send the wrong signal about the kind of experience people were going to have.

Rocky, Marcus' girlfriend and the café manager, had suggested Santa's Village, but Marcus had quashed that idea because it felt confusing to him to have a village within a village, which is basically what our town is. I wouldn't have thought of that dilemma myself, but once he said it, I couldn't help going all meta and imagining Santa in some sort of Escher-like reality where a series of ever-smaller villages sat inside of each other infinitely.

My idea was to go with the classic cottage motif the town had always used, but Rocky and Marcus both said that didn't work because he wasn't really going to have a cottage per se. I briefly wondered about having our friend Woody, the woodsmith, make us a cottage to put in the front of the store, but the logistics of moving around something that big in our small shop made that a no-go. So we were stuck.

And on the Monday after Thanksgiving, we had just five days to decide on a name, make the signs, advertise, and decorate before Santa came for his first evening in the shop on Friday. The three of us were staring into space at one of the café tables, trying to come up with a solution, and it was looking more and more futile. The shop was opening in 15 minutes, and I felt like we had to decide something this morning. We had to pick something, and we'd put it off for as long as we could.

"What if the sign just said, 'Come see Santa?'" Marcus suggested. "Utilitarian but clear."

Rocky sighed. "I guess that would work." She looked at me forlornly.

I echoed her sigh and glanced out the window just in time to see our friend Elle Heron drive by with a child's sled strapped to the top of her minivan. That's when it hit me.

"Santa's Sleigh." I almost whispered.

"What?" Rocky said as she placed her light brown hand over mine. "What did you say?"

I looked from her to Marcus and back. "Santa's Sleigh. What if we set Santa up in a sleigh instead of a chair? That way children could sit next to him if they didn't want to sit on his lap."

Rocky nodded. "Oh, I like that. We want to be sure to keep kids comfortable, and I've always wondered what telling children to sit on a strange man's lap teaches them about their right to say no when it comes to their bodies."

"I agree," and felt my enthusiasm rising as I imagined a bright red sleigh and some Christmas trees around it with that fake snow that had glitter in it. I was just to the point of thinking about how we could string simple white lights around the sleigh to make it light up the store window at night when I caught the expression on Marcus's face. "Oh no. You don't like it?"

He met my gaze. "No, I love it, but I'm remembering this Hall-mark movie, where—"

"Did you say Hallmark Movie?" I smirked.

"Seriously, there's nothing better to put you in the holiday spir-it," he said without a hint of irony. "Great décor. A guaranteed happy ending and just enough drama to keep you interested."

Rocky winked at me. "He's the only black man I know that watches more of them than I do."

"Forget the fact that he's black. He's the only man I know who watches them at all," I laughed as Marcus rolled his eyes. "But you were saying, something about a Hallmark movie." I stuck my tongue out at him.

"I was saying that there's this one movie where they have to find a sleigh for some event at an inn, I think, and they can't find one. Those movies aren't very realistic, but well, that part seems to me as true to life. Where are we going to get a sleigh?"

I felt my excitement deflate. "Good question." I stood up. "Visit Santa it is," I said as I headed toward front of the store, flicked on the open sign, and turned the lock on the door. I tried to counter my disappointment with the excitement I felt about hosting Santa period. But I was still thinking about the sleigh.

Just then, the bell over the front door rang, and Galen – my favorite customer – came in with his English bulldog Mack. My hound Mayhem quickly jogged over, gave Mack the sniff of greeting, and promptly led him to the new couch-shaped dog bed in the fiction section. Galen was always getting doggy goodies because of his Instagram account that featured books and dogs. Apparently, he got so many that he couldn't fit everything in his house, so he gave a lot of it away. For a while, I'd been a grateful beneficiary, but a couple weeks ago, I'd had to tell him that we had now had enough luxury dog beds to sleep 100 dogs and that we had to keep some room for books.

"I was wondering when you'd hit saturation," Galen said with a smile. "Good thing I already lined up my next recipients. Did you know that Cate is now allowing dogs at the co-op?"

My good friend Cate was a photographer and the owner of the amazing art co-op at the other end of Main Street. Her dog Sasquatch was another of Mayhem's buds. "I didn't know that. I thought she was worried about fur in the clay and the paint and such."

"She was, but then Sasquatch was feeling sick one day and had to come to work with her. She put his doggy bed in the window, and their traffic doubled. So she polled the artists. Turns out, everyone was in favor." Galen grinned as he looked over at Mayhem and Mack, who were butt to butt on their couch.

"I told her, but I guess she had to see for herself." A good point of our foot traffic came in because the dogs especially loved the sunshine in the front windows in the afternoon. "I'm glad you can pass along your goodies to someone else then. You have a lot of space there, too."

"Yep, one bed per artist and a few for the lobby, I figure." Galen was staring over at Mack with such gentle adoration. Dog people were special, and not all of us carried our dogs in purses .

. . although I couldn't really resist those teacup chihuahuas that customers brought in from time to time.

"So what's new around here? Anything you want me to Insta for the holidays?"

I groaned. Audibly and Galen raised his eyebrows. "We were just talking about that. Santa is going to be here for the weekends starting this Friday, but we haven't figured out what to call his, well, place." I sighed. "Cottage doesn't work, and village feels weird. We talked about a sleigh, but then we couldn't figure out how to get a sleigh—"

"I have a sleigh you can use."

"So we're going with a sign that says . . . wait, what?!" It took my brain a few seconds to stop my mouth. "Did you say you have a sleigh?"

"Yep. I put it in the front yard with a bunch of life-sized stuffed dogs to pull it, but I'm kind of tired of hauling the thing out, and last year, a squirrel made a nest in the Great Pyrenees belly. So I wasn't planning on using it this year. It's yours if you want it."

I stared at Galen for a long moment, picturing the sleigh with a dog team pulling it and then the squirrel climbing out of a fake Great Pyr belly before I finally registered that he had just solved our problem. "Really?! That would be amazing. Are you sure?"

"Absolutely. Maybe Daniel can come by and get it?" Galen said.

"Sure. I mean I'll ask, but I expect he'd be happy to. Will it fit in my truck?" I drove an old model Chevy, and I loved it. But it wasn't one of these honking things that can carry two round bales of hay that some folks around here drove.

Galen smiled. "It's actually on a trailer already. I keep it on there to make it easier to move in and out of the garage, and it's not very heavy. So I think your girl could tow it over just fine."

I shook my hips in a little happy dance. "You just saved Christmas, Galen."

He blushed and said, "No, no . . . I'm just glad the sleigh is going to get used."

I hugged him tight, and his blush got deeper against his steel-gray hair. "Want to be an elf?" I asked with a wink.

He held one leg out suggestively and said, "I do look good in tights. But no thanks." He winked. "I will come by and take a few pics, though, if that's okay."

"More than okay. And your next stack of books is on me. Call it a rental fee."

"Deal," he said and held out his hand to shake. "Come by whenever for the sleigh. I'll text you the address."

"Perfect. Thank you again," I said and squealed. "Santa's Sleigh Ride is a go!"

BY FRIDAY NIGHT, Galen's Instagram promotion, the really amazing window display that Marcus had created, and the sleigh itself had drummed up some big interest in Santa's first night. Fortunately, my parents had offered to host Thanksgiving. Otherwise, Mart, Daniel, and I would probably have had a bag of Bugles, a can of spray cheese, and a bottle of wine for our meal. We were all slammed with holiday prep – Mart at the winery where she worked and Daniel with me at the store, where he was recruited to hang lights and help stock the shelves with the year's hottest titles. Books had always been big sellers during the December holidays, and I wanted to be prepared for even more sales this year.

We had been closed for Thanksgiving, but we opened early on Friday morning with our Black Friday discount of buy three books in one genre get one free. The sale only lasted until 10am, and then we went to a straight 10% off everything until Santa arrived at 4pm.

I'd taken a little inspiration from Galen and arranged an entourage of dogs to "pull" his sleigh for the first customers who arrived, and when a tiny girl with braids and beads in her hair came in the door, she screamed with delight as did her mother. "Doggies," she said. "Black Santa," was her mother's joyful sentiment. We were off to a great start.

Soon, the line of folks with their kiddos was out the door, and I realized that I was going to have to serve as the elf and keep the line moving. If I could have, I would have let each and every child sit for as long - or as short - a time as they wanted, but it soon became clear I was going to have to set a time limit or plan to be here well past midnight. I enlisted Marcus's help, and he drew a quick sign that said, "Santa's legs get tired. Please limit your visits to 2 requests and 3 minutes each." That helped some, but of course, some folks also needed to be ushered along with a gentle hand under the elbow.

Mayhem and Mac, our lead "rein-dogs" were holding steady at the front of the lines, but behind them, most of the other pooches, including Cate's restless Schauzner Sasquatch and Mack, were getting restless. So at six, I sent the pups on their way with bags of treats and my hearty thanks, and we went dogless for the rest of the evening.

Just before 9, we were getting ready to close up, and I was about to fall over from fatigue. Supervising a line of children was exhausting, but it was the persnickety attitudes of some of the parents that were really draining. I simply could *not* with the mother who insisted that her child go back to Santa because she has not requested the right American Girl doll, and the father who felt like his son shouldn't ask for a teddy bear because it was too much of a sissy gift got a stern glare from me and a free copy of *When The Bees Fly Home* to help him and his gorgeous son explore those awful gender stereotypes.

The event had been great, but I was making a little list of things we needed - bottles of water for staff and people in line, a chair for the resident elf, more resident elfs - when I saw that the last person in line was a grown man without any children. I kept an eye out, wondering if maybe the child in question was in the restroom, but when he finally made it to Santa, he was still alone. Alone and swaying on his feet.

I gave Marcus a quick wave, and he came over, seeing immediately the issue at hand, and helped me steady our final guest as he reached Santa. I looked at Damien, our Santa, with the obvious question in my eyes, and he took a deep breath before nodding. Then, this thin but very tall white man slumped down into Santa's lap.

"What can Santa do for you this year, er, young man?" Damien boomed in his best Santa voice.

The guy in his lap was now leaning against Damien's chest, and even when Damien jostled around, the guy didn't move. I groaned, and Marcus and I each took one of the guy's arms and pulled him upright off of Damien's lap. But the guy didn't even attempt to hold his own weight. He went right past vertical and slammed into the table in front of him.

For a split second, I continued to think he was drunk until I realized that he hadn't made even a grunt when his nose had smacked into the table top nor when his shoulder had slammed into the floor. "Oh no," I said with horror.

Damien knelt down and put his fingers to the guy's neck. When he wasn't moonlighting as Santa, Damien was a volunteer firefighter and had some medical training. "No pulse. Call 911."

Then, Damien flipped the guy onto his back and started chest compressions as Marcus moved to the man's head, presumably to give him mouth-to-mouth.

For a second, I just stood there, staring, but then I jarred myself into action and dialed.

By the time the ambulance arrived, it was clear this guy wasn't waking up. Someone had died, in Santa's lap, in my bookstore, on the first day of the Christmas season.

Tome To Tomb **is coming in November. Pre-order your copy here to read more - books2read.com/tometotomb.**

HARVEY AND MARCUS'S BOOK RECOMMENDATIONS

Here, you will find all the books and authors recommended in *Plotted For Murder* to add to your never-ending to-read-list!

- *How Many Seeds in a Pumpkin* by Margaret McNamara
- *Pumpkin It Up* by Eliza Cross
- *Apple Caramel Mayhem* by Leena Clover
- *Blue Moon* by Lee Child
- *My Sister, The Serial Killer* by Oyinkan Baithwite
- *The Body Keeps The Score* by Bessel van der Kolk
- *Why Does He Do That?* by Lundy Bancroft
- *The Complete Illustrated Book of Herbs* by Readers' Digest
- *Running Rewired* by Jay DiCharry
- *Yarned and Dangerous* by Sadie Hartwell
- *Ghost Academy* by E. C. Farrell
- *A Rule Against Murder* by Louise Penny
- *The Joy Luck Club* by Amy Tan
- *The Watchmen* by Alan Moore
- *Sailor Moon* by Naoko Takeuchi
- *Andy Goldsworthy: Projects* by Andy Goldsworthy
- *The Summer House* by James Patterson

- *Warrior Cats: Into The Wild* by Erin Hunter
- *Gray's Anatomy* by Henry Gray
- *The Body in the Bookmobile* by Connie B. Dowell
- *Wild* by Cheryl Strayed
- *Just Mercy* by Bryan Stevenson
- *The New Jim Crow* by Michelle Alexander
- *Speaking Truth To Power* by Anita Hill
- *Not That Bad* by Roxane Gay
- *We Believe You* by Annie E. Clark and Andrea L. Pino
- *The Courage To Heal* by Ellen Bass

I recommend these books highly. Feel free to drop me a line at acfbookens@andilit.com and let me know if you read any or have books you think I should read. Thanks!

Happy Reading,

ACF

WANT TO READ ABOUT HARVEY'S FIRST SLEUTHING EXPEDITION?

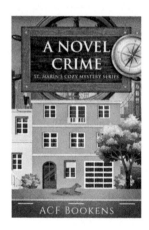

Join my Cozy Up email group for weekly book recs & a FREE copy of *A Novel Crime*, the prequel to the St. Marin's Cozy Mystery Series.

Sign-up here - https://bookens.andilit.com/CozyUp

ALSO BY ACF BOOKENS

St. Marin's Cozy Mystery Series

Publishable By Death

Entitled To Kill

Bound To Execute

Plotted For Murder

Tome To Tomb

Scripted To Slay

Proof Of Death

Stitches In Crime Series

Crossed By Death

Bobbins and Bodies

Hanged By A Thread

ABOUT THE AUTHOR

ACF Bookens lives in the Blue Ridge Mountains of Virginia, where the mountain tops remind her that life is a rugged beauty of a beast worthy of our attention. When she's not writing, she enjoys watching her young son climb *everything*, cross-stitching while she binge-watches police procedurals, and reading everything she can get her hands on. Find her at bookens.andilit.com.

facebook.com/BookensCozyMysteries

Printed in Great Britain
by Amazon

80750256R00120